Also by Salvatore La Puma

The Boys of Bensonhurst: Stories
A Time for Wedding Cake

TEACHING ANGELS TO FLY

W · W · NORTON & COMPANY · NEW YORK · LONDON

TEACHING ANGELS TO FLY

STORIES BY Salvatore La Puma

All the characters in these stories are fictitious,
and any resemblance to persons living or dead is coincidental.

Printed in the United States of America
First Edition

The text of this book is composed in Garamond No. 3
with the display set in Futura Bold Italic
Composition and manufacturing by The Maple-Vail Manufacturing Group
Book design by Antonina Krass

Library of Congress Cataloging-in-Publication Data

La Puma, Salvatore.
Teaching angels to fly / by Salvatore La Puma.
p. cm.
I. Title.
PS3562.A15T4 1992
813'.54—dc20 91-36434

ISBN 0-393-03358-9

W.W. Norton & Company, Inc., 500 Fifth Avenue, New York, N.Y. 10110
W.W. Norton & Company Ltd., 10 Coptic Street, London WC1A 1PU

1 2 3 4 5 6 7 8 9 0

For Charles East,
Mary Evans, and
Gerald Howard

CONTENTS

TEACHING ANGELS TO FLY

LIGHTNING

On the roof is where I find her. "Lucky it's the roof and not the street," she says. "With the traffic down there, there's hardly room to land on my feet." She sits with her legs out while I stand above her. Her face comes out of the shadows to look up. All that I can see before her head pulls into the dark again is that she is very young with big slanted eyes. Why is she up here alone, when, besides, a storm is coming? To jump off the roof? Or, like me, just to see the lightning?

The night sky is jigsawed by the lightning. It might, for an hour, charge up my dull life. The lightning is beautiful, but deadly too. Maybe, when it is closer, when I go back down, it will strike her if it is her intention to reach up for it. When it flashes now, there is enough light to stare at each other. She doesn't have much on. Actually, she is wearing sort of a costume. It is made up of scarves in all colors which billow in the wind. Like a father I want to cover her with a blanket. But I also want to look at her.

"I'm sorry I tripped on your feet," I say.

"I have big feet," she replies. "Big feet are supposed to be good to land on, see, but I'm also a little clumsy." She giggles. "Here, in the dark, I was trying to stay out of the way, but in this city, even the rooftops are crowded."

"It could rain any minute," I say. "If you count the seconds between the lightning and the thunder, you can tell the storm's getting closer."

"It's a pretty good storm," she says, "coming up from the south."

I squat down to speak to the shadow that she herself is inside the shadow made by the shed for the door to the roof. "Are you up here alone?"

"My mother was with me. But she didn't know what to do, so she went to fetch Zeke."

Maybe her mother went for help to get her daughter off the roof. Maybe I can talk her off the roof. "Do you live in the building? I don't remember seeing you. Possibly in one of the other buildings? Is something wrong? Is there something I can do to help?"

"It isn't that easy." Her head pokes out to where I can see a wing on each shoulder. The wings seem made of cardboard and decorated with sequins. She points to the wing on the right shoulder. "It was singed by a lightning bolt." She giggles again. "It tickled. And it bent the wing so I had to make a forced landing."

They are big wings which I doubt would float in the air even if they could be flapped. "Here, put my raincoat around your shoulders," I say, and then put it around her myself. "Where did you get the wings?"

"Down south in a wonderful place," she says.

Her voice makes a beautiful sound. Sonia's voice also makes a beautiful sound. In two weeks I will be married to Sonia. Sonia herself is a young woman, but not this young. Understandably, Sonia wouldn't want me to rescue another young woman. But I have to do it. I can't stand by and allow this young woman to possibly harm herself.

"You have, I'd say, a faint regional accent, possibly North Carolina. I think I remember, when I was in the army, that my company commander was from North Carolina. I was in for two years. Now I'm a pharmacist. I have a small drugstore on Prince Street. So, am I right? Is it North Carolina?"

"You have a wonderful ear," she says. "Yes, you see, it was where I received my wings. In the hills of North Carolina near Cricket. You know how it is when you apply for a job—you make out the application, you interview, you orientate, you train, and finally, you go to work; by that time, you pick up all the jargon, or, in my case, the accent. It can be at a training center anywhere—North Carolina, San Francisco, even two in Antarctica. It's where angels learn to fly."

"Look, my apartment is down on the fourth floor," I say. "You can put on my Chinese robe. It's blue, silky stuff, with white dragons."

"Is this a come-on?" she says.

"No, I don't think so. You can't be more than twenty, or twenty-one."

"Three," she says.

"Okay. I'm forty-one, much too old for you. It's just not safe for you up here, with the lightning, besides, getting closer, the wind picking up."

"I've never been to a man's apartment before." She stands up. She is very tall, and beautiful, dark and beautiful; dark, I think, from the night's shadows.

"It's two flights down," I say, as we go downstairs.

When she looks back to say, "You won't chase me around the bed will you," I see her dark eyes filled with tiny stars. "With a broken wing, you know, I can't exactly fly out the window."

"We'll just get you the robe," I say. "And see if we can fix that wing. Maybe a little rubber cement."

"My name is Uriel." She beams at me. "What's yours?"

I have to beam at her too, as I say, "Wally Calhoun."

"Well, Wally, I hope rubber cement does the trick. Zeke, you know, has this sticky tape to patch up wings and feet." In the apartment the raincoat seems to lift off her shoulders before it drops to the floor behind her. Then she plops down on the sofa and stretches out.

"Why don't you put this on?" I hand her the blue robe. "Don't you attract too much attention just in scarves? They are scarves, aren't they?"

"Well, yes, but these scarves have a certain buoyancy; like balloons, they always want to go up."

"They don't exactly cover your legs," I say.

Uriel sits up and slips into the robe. "If it makes you feel better, Wally, I'll put it on." Then she fixes me in her gaze. "I think, Wally, that you think that maybe I'm high on something."

"It did occur to me, yes, but you also seem not high; you seem fairly normal, except for the wings."

"Perhaps, Wally, it's you who is high. Perhaps I'm just in your mind."

"Uriel, if I could've dreamed you up before tonight, I surely would have. Would you mind if I touch you, just to be positive I'm not high?"

"Touch this hand," she says.

"It's a very pretty hand."

"That, I'm sure, is a come-on."

"I didn't mean it that way. Would you like me to come on to you?"

"Well, it would be interesting. But if I liked it, it could get us both in a lot of trouble." Then she covers both ears. "It must be Zeke at the door."

The knocks come again. But I don't make a move to ask who is there. "How would Zeke know you're in my apartment?" This moment shouldn't be interrupted.

"We should let him in," Uriel says. "He has an awful temper. It's his one failing. We all have one failing. Otherwise, we would be saints. You know what mine is?"

"Your feet?"

"No, we all have big feet. It's good to have big feet. My failing is curiosity."

"I thought curiosity was a good thing," I say.

The knocks on the door are louder.

"Well, yes, curiosity is good, if you're curious, Zeke says, about the right things. But, see, I'm curious about you too, and that's a wrong thing for me to be curious about." She pouts, beautifully. "I think you'd better let Zeke in. Otherwise, he might come through the window."

"It's four flights up. He can't."

She giggles and runs to the door and throws it open.

"Mother! We were *just talking.*"

Uriel's mother is about my own age. But she is also mostly undressed. So I dash back for the white terry robe, shorter for summer. The mother takes it. She looks it over. Then hands it back.

"We don't take gifts," she says.

"There's an awful chill out tonight," I say. "It's the end of September."

"That's thoughtful of you." She sits on the sofa beside her daughter. "I suppose, Uriel, you're attracted to him because he's thoughtful."

"He offered to fix my wing," Uriel says.

"Well, then, mister, let's see you fix Uriel's wing."

I get the rubber cement from the desk in the kitchen where I work on the books some evenings, where I pay bills and seal envelopes. Uriel closes her dark slanted eyes and her head tilts forward to bring her wings closer. They even feel like cardboard. And the shiny little red and blue disks really feel like sequins. Still, I go along with it. I glue a small strip of shirt cardboard over the crease in the right wing. After I hold the patch in place for two minutes, the cement dries. When I let go, the wing stands up like the other one. Uriel reaches around to feel that it's no longer floppy.

"You're simply wonderful, Wally. I bet not many men nowadays can fix a broken wing."

"It's no big deal, Uriel."

"Listen, mister, nice as you may be, don't get any ideas. My daughter has her life cut out for her."

"I wasn't thinking anything like that."

"You'd only be disappointed anyway." To her daughter she

says, "It's time, baby, that we leave here. Zeke said to meet him on 42nd Street. He has a lot of people to patch up."

"Must we really go, mother? It's so cozy in here."

"It's him, isn't it? You're interested in this man. Would you give up your perfect life just to be with this man?"

"It does seem dumb," Uriel says.

"Well, fortunately for you, baby, I'm here to save you from that mistake." The mother turns to me.

"Just pretend you dreamed all this, okay?" She opens a window, climbs out to sit on the ledge, and disappears.

"I have to go too," Uriel says, and the blue robe falls to the floor. "Tomorrow, after the storm, you'll be surprised at what a bright shiny day it'll be." Then she sits on the ledge and touches the restored wing again. "You fixed it really good. Thanks."

"Any chance, Uriel, you can come back here? Just to talk?"

"You'll have Sonia by then. She'll be your wife."

"How do you know about Sonia?" I ask.

"Wally, see, we know a few things. And she's very nice."

"Yes," I say, "she is very nice."

"Maybe once in a while," Uriel says, "I'll just peek in your window." Then she slips off the ledge and is gone.

THE FOUR OF US

He was standing there like the shower curtain, so straight and still," Lisa says. "And so pale."

Lisa and Ken can't be held accountable for meeting in the bathroom in the dark. But they have to give up on each other someday soon. There's no other choice. Until then, I have to sweat it out. Still, to encourage her to push Ken out the door for good, I say, "Lisa, I'm really tired of Ken coming here."

"When I got up to get a drink of water," she says, "there he was, in the bathroom." Now her face brightens. "But listen, Tony," she says, "he really wasn't *in* the bathroom." She taps a painted fingernail on her head. "It's really in here I saw him, not *in there.*"

"Why do you have to see him *at all?*" I say in a voice I usually use when my sixth-graders get out of hand. "At night when *I* go to the bathroom, I never find Jessie in there. Jessie stays exactly where she is. So it's hard to understand why Ken can't stay exactly where he is."

Her orange-pink fingernails gather a sheer stocking into soft folds. She holds the stocking and sits in a chair on her side of the bed, then points one foot into the stocking. Orange-pink are her toenails too. For years, for Ken, she said, she painted her toenails, until Ken no longer noticed them. For me, I said, Jessica, too, had painted her toenails until I no longer noticed them. Now Lisa paints hers again. And I notice them again.

Weekday mornings Lisa is all business diving into pants and sweaters, rushing off to third grade at Peabody School, where I teach too. But this morning, as on most other Sunday mornings, Lisa, putting on her clothes, is as erotic as a burlesque queen. To move myself closer to her, I drop crosswise on the bed. The bed is from when she was married to Ken. It has a high headboard with an outer rail of walnut rising to a rounded peak. The center is tufted in a small Victorian print. The mattress, too, is great—nice and firm. So when we first moved in together, I didn't say we had to have a new bed. It was where we first made love. And its prior history never held us back.

"It's about the fourth time," I say, "you've seen Ken in this apartment." I try to look serious as I lie across the bed looking at her putting on her stockings. But I'm afraid the pleasure I feel is revealed in my voice. "Lisa, I can't believe he followed you *here.* He never lived *here.* If he absolutely has to come back, I'd think, where he lived last would be where he'd come back."

"Tony, you can't be jealous. It's Ken who has a right to be jealous," she says. "Ken said last night he can't understand why, just six weeks after he was gone, we found each other." In her mid-thirties Lisa still has a child's round face, and when it suits her purpose, like now, she erases from that face all her thoughts and feelings, as from a blackboard, and puts on a mask of child-like innocence. I'm never convinced of her innocence, but I always like to look at her innocent face. It disarms me of my suspicions, which burden me more than they do her.

"The next time you see him, Lisa, why don't you just wake me up," I say and pout. "Maybe, for coming here, I'll take a swing at him." I'm not sure if I'm kidding or not.

"Tony, to get Jessie out of your own head, you had two whole years," Lisa says. "Although, often enough, it seems to me, Jessie, too, is right here. Right here in the middle of our conversation. Do you think I'm *eager* to hear about Jessie? Even those comparisons where she fails, I'm not thrilled to hear about." Now Lisa, too, pouts. "Instead of two of us, Tony, it's the four of us who seem to live here." Her stockings snapped on, she goes to the closet, undecided between a red blouse to go with a black leather skirt, or a white blouse with a beige wool skirt.

Lisa is solidly in my life. There's no doubt about it. Yet I still want her as if there is still more to want. It isn't that she holds anything back. Everything Lisa is Lisa gives to me. She even tells me things she didn't tell Ken: when she at twelve broke her mother's antique Chinese vase, it was on purpose; when years ago it was suddenly clear as water to her why her older brother who crushes my hand in a handshake has never had a girlfriend. After Lisa empties herself out, I know a little more about her. The next day she's filled up again with new things to say simply because, she says, "You, Tony, want to hear it all."

The red blouse is it. And I go to button her up just for the pleasure of standing close to her, and to play a part in the show business of her dressing herself. Then, to let in the morning air, I open the windows and prop open one window with a book. From our upstairs rooms in this old Mediterranean-style apartment house from which terra-cotta roof tiles sometimes fly off in heavy winds, I look down on Garden Street and neighbors headed for church.

Then I help Lisa make the bed.

We go out and stroll to Figueroa Street to Angelo's Pastry Shop. At a small round marble table, we peel fresh tangerines and eat cannoli. And have two cups of black coffee each, two cubes of sugar in each cup, laced with a shot of anisette.

Then we amble down toward the beach, toward Cabrillo Boulevard, where, on Saturdays and Sundays, there's something called Sabado Domingo, a lot of arts and crafts. To go for a walk with Lisa is a married thing to do even though we're both uncertain we want to get married again.

We hold hands and window-shop and look around at the tourists. We talk about kids in our classes and try to figure them out. When now we stop at a dress-shop window, Lisa says, "That's a color I like—a sort of peeled peach. Isn't it a wonderful color for summer? I have to get some new summer dresses. Along with Ken's clothes, I gave away most of my own."

"Did you really care about Ken, I mean, a lot?" I say, for the hundredth time.

"Tony, I didn't even kiss another man in the nine years we were married. Yes, of course, I cared about Ken," she says in a low voice, "and deeply too." Then she cheers up to add, "But it was different than it is for us. It wasn't as steamy."

"Do you think, Lisa, that you could avoid seeing him when

I'm asleep at night? It sort of bothers me," I say. "I know it's foolish of me, the guy gone and all, but could you?"

"If he shows up again, I'll call you, Tony. And you can tell him to leave. Okay?" To reassure me now, she kisses my cheek. Then we cross the street in front of traffic at the light. "You might even tell him," she says, "he has your permission, if he feels he needs it, to look Jessie up, if he can find her. There must be skillions of souls over there. It must be like at the Rose Bowl, a mob scene. If, in fact," she says, stopping for eye contact, "you yourself can let go of Jessie. And it's *me* you want to spend eternity with."

"For all I care, he can have Jessie. It's just fine with me," I say. But there's a shiver on my spine. It isn't that I still want Jessie. It's Lisa I want. But I'm not sure I want to hand Jessie over to Ken.

"I'm not sure Ken would want Jessie," I say. "She isn't his type. She crunched numbers and only believed in what came up on her screen. Your Ken was an actor," I say with a hint of dislike, "and even now he's trying to steal the show. However, Lisa—and you can tell him yourself—if he wants her, and she wants him, they have my blessing."

"Mine too," Lisa says.

Now she begins to step up the pace. "At Domino's should we have anchovies or mozzarella?"

"Would it be excessive," I say, "to have both?"

SAILING

"They played horsy," Jill says, as Carter Avis comes in in his whites, his blue blazer draped down one shoulder. It appears the downpour hasn't fallen on him. On his pants are only a few fringed water marks. To the little girl he doesn't say a word. He just sidesteps her, then takes long lopes to the dining room. Jill races after him. "Daddy, they played horsy." On the dining table her eyeless doll reclaims her attention. She climbs up on a chair, hugs the doll hard, then pokes a finger in each empty eye socket.

After two swift scotches, his shoulders square up and he sails toward Ondine's voice. "Carter, we're in here," she calls.

Ondine waits in a wing chair. Her head tilts to the side to raise for him her left cheek. It receives Carter's boozy kiss. From another wing chair Lenny rises, buttons his jacket, holds out his hand.

"Who are you?" Carter, very tall, lengthens out even more. "Do I know you?" Has he forgotten this man? They shake hands.

Lenny, of average size, shrinks in his shoes. Then grins like an old buddy. "Lenny Tucci." He looks to Ondine to explain why he is here. "You don't know me personally."

"I'd like to say," Carter says, "that you look familiar." To forecast his sly good humor his mouth puckers. "But I can't tell what you look like under that beard." He drops himself into a big chair.

Jill and her sister Nancy sit on a Persian rug in the center. Jill has on a short fluffy plum dress tied with a big white bow in back. Nancy, a long peach dress with a high waist. Both wear white tights and black maryjanes. Their nails, which are painted their mother's nail color, compete to poke in the doll's eye sockets.

"Carter, he's the fellow who did the canvas"—Ondine's voice hints that he should have known what she's about to say—"your birthday present." In the pause Carter brightens. She breezes on. "I thought since you like the painting so much, you'd like to meet Lenny Tucci in person."

"But I wasn't here," he says, as a thought clouds his face. "I was on the boat. Why is he here when only you're here?" He leaves the room to return with another drink. As he sits down again one long leg swings over the other.

Ondine, too, crosses her legs. Then tucks the hem of her flowered dress over her knees. "When I heard this morning's weather report"—her matter-of-fact tone defies his disbelief—"I just knew, Carter, that you'd be back, the latest by afternoon. So I called Mr. Tucci, to surprise you." Her expression is thoughtful and calm. "We hoped you'd be back for lunch. We had a light lunch with Jill and Nancy. Yellow tomatoes and little sandwiches Ruby made. We saved some for you." She gets up and goes to Carter, whose brushed-back blond hair she combs with long red fingernails. "Have something to eat, dear. I'll bring in a plate you can have here while you talk." She turns to Lenny. "Carter has two degrees in art history. He could have a top spot at a museum."

"Nothing to eat, thanks," Carter says. A motion of his hand sends her back to her chair, where she sits down again.

Ondine still hopes that Carter will straighten out. Sometimes his looks are still elegant. Sometimes his brain is still quick. Sometimes his feet on the dance floor still have wings. He is never bad to her. And he loves his little girls. His life must be saved. To abandon him is unthinkable. A burden she doesn't want is to raise the girls without him. His daughters need their father's applause.

Carter talks about how the storm rocked the boat. How the waves washed over it. The work the hull needs to get the boat shipshape. In three weeks it sails down the Hudson to blue water and Block Island.

"The girls won't be happy an entire day on the boat, another day coming back," Ondine says. "I myself, Carter, have other things to do." His plan to go sailing often brings on her tug-of-war. Through the years she has pulled harder against sailing. "I thought it was all settled about the trip," she says. "That we wouldn't go, that you wouldn't go either."

When no one speaks now the absence of sound strengthens for Lenny the smell of incense in the air. It was burned in the fireplace when the gas log was lit. The absence of talk also gives Nancy, six, her chance to speak up. She sits cross-legged on the rug. Her dress is hiked to her knees. "They played cowboy," Nancy announces.

Jill, with both her knees now down on the rug, is in the crouch of a crapshooter. She is younger and smaller. But she won't be outdone. She was the first to peek through a crack in the bedroom door. First to name the game the grown-ups played. So now she has the right to correct Nancy. Her neck stretches. "Horsy—they played horsy."

As soon as their reports are tossed off to their father, the girls then compete to kiss the doll to console it for the lost eyes which they earlier took out.

"What in blazes," Carter asks Ondine, "are they talking about?"

"Those wonderful cowboy outfits you bought them. Well, I showed them to Mr. Tucci." Ondine is serene. It makes her, Lenny observes, a wonderful liar. "With his niece about to have her fifth birthday, he asked if I could suggest something."

The elaborate lie doesn't answer Carter's question. It pretends to answer it. It also suggests to Lenny Ondine's quick and devious mind. In years to come he can hear himself say. "That's a lie, Ondine." He will say it if they come together, even if she doesn't leave Carter. The lie will echo in his memory down the years. He will never be completely convinced she will always tell him the truth.

Puzzled by Ondine's explanation, Carter gazes at Lenny. Then back at Ondine. "I see," he says flatly. His thin dry lips smile a little to apologize for his sudden inquisitor's squint. It may be as she says—that Lenny is here as a surprise for him. But Carter hasn't taken her to bed in a year. And hopes no one else will either. If she can just be patient a little longer she will be wanted that way again. His habit won't have to be given up. He can't quite yet give it up. It makes his life right now more interesting. What he has to do is to focus on his virility. When he dreams, a little tent in the bedsheet sometimes goes up. His doctor says it's a start. So Ondine has to be kept pristine to be made full use of any day now as he himself keeps pristine for her.

"If you'll excuse me a minute," Carter says. What Ondine possibly did he shuts out of his thoughts. He doesn't want to think about it now. "When I come back, Mr. Tucci, I'd like to know what's behind those shapes in that canvas of yours. The one Ondine bought."

"Call me Lenny."

"Fine, Lenny. I'll be right back, Lenny." Carter charts a course for the hallway bathroom.

Lenny and Ondine look away from each other to deny their conspiracy. Ondine looks instead at the blue flames in the fireplace. Lenny, at the ridges in the picture molding on the walls near the ceiling. Then both look at the cute little stool pigeons on the rug who might still spoil it all.

"What he's doing in there," says Ondine, "is taking a hit."

Five minutes later Carter comes back. His mouth seems satisfied and his eyes lit. But there are still shadows around his eyes. "I see that in the bathroom," Carter says with pleasure, "the girls had another water fight."

Water pistols and cowboy outfits were his birthday gifts. Ondine said she wouldn't have approved of them even for sons. For Carter, guns have always been for rabbit, for skeet, and later for Canadian caribou. Shotguns etched with gold, ancient pistols handmade, were handed down in his family, along with works of art, rugs, and furniture.

"Yes, Lenny, I do like that canvas," Carter says. "Real things on canvas by now bore me. What shapes and design stand for in your mind, and what they become for me, those are puzzles in which I feel involved. And colors. Give me unexpected colors that come together in a way not seen before, and I'll look at them for days. You know what I mean."

"I know what you mean." Lenny is aware that here is another Carter. This Carter wouldn't now ask questions to be answered with other lies, or with the painful truth.

"Art is more important than life." Carter is pleased about this insight which might please Lenny. It's what critics write and gallery owners whisper; and what collectors repeat. But Lenny thinks they are wrong—life is more important than art.

"I think, Carter, that we are two of a kind here," Lenny says. He almost has to like this guy who himself seems at sea. Carter is in desperate need of being saved. But saved from what? Does Carter himself know?

Down on the rug the little girls tire of the doll. And shove each other. Nancy stands up, pouts with hands on hips, then snatches up the doll too. Before she can run off with it, Jill pulls the semisoft legs out of the hip sockets. To retrieve them Nancy bends over at the waist. In that position she inspires Jill to get up to stand behind her, to loop her arms around her, to once again say, "Horsy. Mommy and him played horsy."

There it is acted out. And Ondine doesn't come up with another lie. The truth spoken by little girls seems to be as close as one on earth can get to the truth. Lenny feebly shakes his head. In a year or two, maybe, they will learn from older kids, from Ondine and Carter, how to lie. For now they are all stuck with their certain truth.

Carter's shined-up eyes now scrutinize Ondine's face. Then Lenny's face. There are other facts to determine. Was it good between them? Was it the first or hundredth time? It is a moment Carter has long worried about. But hasn't prepared for. How could he? He couldn't have guessed how he would feel. Now he knows. Anger rises up from his middle. Comes into his hands. Into his mind. Into his silent mouth. Then his arms and knees shake. Quickly he forces himself out of the room as the shakes get worse.

Lenny thinks he himself should now make a run for it. They can fight it out themselves. It really isn't his fight. Carter might even take a punch at him. Which could make Carter feel better. Then Ondine won't get punched. Or Lenny himself might take a swing at Carter. Then Carter can feel better as a victim in spades. So Lenny waits to see if the situation will worsen or simmer down.

In two minutes Carter is back. "I'm going to kill you, Ondine." He aims a huge handgun with a dark blue barrel.

Self-control that doesn't fail her at possibly this last moment of her life allows Ondine to say, "Why kill me, Carter?" Her long painted fingers curl around the barrel. She redirects it at Lenny. "The wronged husband is supposed to shoot the other man. Not his wife. He still loves his wife. Don't you, Carter, still love me? I still love you."

"It's a man's instinct to screw an attractive woman," fumes Carter. "But, first, and this is important, Ondine—so pay attention—he waits for her consent. Without her consent he doesn't make a move. You didn't have to give your consent."

"It's been, you know, a long time, Carter. I was afraid you'd forgotten how." Her voice gets stronger. She is indignant she is held accountable. "I had to give my consent. I thought, Carter, you wouldn't ever want to again."

"Say your prayers, Ondine." Flushing, Carter hunches slightly, the gun inches from her pretty face. "Yes, I still love you, Ondine. Which is why I have to shoot you. Then you'll be dead. Everyone knows it's ridiculous to love someone who's dead."

"Not in front of the children." Ondine's fingers firmly turn the barrel aside. She stands. Then strides out of the room. And after her scamper the little girls, the doll left behind on the rug.

Carter and Lenny glare at each other. Then Jill and Nancy return. In their hands are their plastic pistols. Bubbles visible inside the pistols show them to be almost fully loaded. The girls seem to take their example from their father, who still holds the big handgun down by his side. They begin to shoot the two men with blue water from the toilet bowl. Their prime target is their father. It is a massacre of blue blood by blue blood. Less often are their guns squirted at Lenny. Like most children, Lenny thinks, the little girls save their deadliest shots for those who love them most.

PHOTOGRAPH

Boy have I some rotten news for you.

A son dressed as a pirate bringing his father bad news will be thrown to the sharks.

Maybe I should write you a letter you're in no condition to hear it out loud you might have a heart attack the way you look Dad.

Don't worry about me born with almost brass knuckles on a street where you made it or moved.

You said you moved Dad.

Well maybe I'm not so tough but I can take it whatever you did bad. You're only a kid Paul who wouldn't do anything really bad. So what is it—dealing dope drunk driving what?

Nothing easy as that but the bad news has a good side too a fantastic good side to drool over knowing how you feel about a buck not making one putting people to sleep these days.

When I get back on my feet I'll send them to dreamland again to get sliced up like cold cuts tell me the good news first.

It's your lucky day Dad—no more support payments—don't you just want to cheer your brains out?

No more payments my God did she die?

She didn't die she's losing weight and getting younger every day and any minute could turn into my sister.

Thank God she didn't die I couldn't stand her leaving a second time.

If you want to know the truth it's worse than that I'm sorry to say you ready for this?

She's going with some guy in gold chains?

Not only she's going with but marrying besides how'd you know the dude wore gold chains?

Impossible Paul I don't believe the woman I've known all these years would.

The crows she said are crash-landing on her face and time's running out you know to who Dad? The dude owns the Biltmore a radio station a yacht he'll take me on someday to Tortuga Island where pirates hanged out.

I hope she'll be very happy even though it takes a lot to make her happy.

He's so rich she'll live like a rock star so maybe I'll go live with her.

I won't eat at the Biltmore anymore.

You never eat at the Biltmore.

I ate across the street from it once.

She's inviting you besides to the wedding on Saturday and was going to ask you to give her away but I said you already did and she'd be pushing her luck since you said you could kill her.

Not in the flesh Paul just kill her in my head.

So you're going to the wedding she asked me too I'm not I hate weddings somebody walking the plank is what I'd like to see.

I'm not going either Paul but I would've gone to her funeral. I'm surprised she didn't tell me herself on the phone yesterday when she called.

She said she didn't have the heart so she asked me to you know how parents lean on us kids all the time.

My wife in bed with another man.

Think of the alimony add it up you'll save a million dollars.

Twelve hundred a month times 12 months a year times 12 years I forget the times tables Paul.

Dad forget Mom let me tell you about Simone's mom Simone's this cute girl up the block. Her mom said I have a great chin do you get it Dad? My cleft is your cleft so suppose I bring Simone and her mom over some night for an orgy?

An orgy will stunt your growth Paul you should think about winning a bike race at your age not an orgy.

Somebody's going to think you're dead sitting there like that if you don't have an orgy pretty soon Dad and when I'm not around somebody's going to shovel dirt in your face.

Is he younger taller better-looking?

Wears these great threads no pockets which fit like skin really hip man. Not one extra hair or ounce and diamond teeth that shine right in your eye.

Why would he want your mother?

He said he's crazy about her brownies.

I should've had her brownies but they always came out too raw.

Simone's mom makes great cookies Dad you ought to taste

her cookies really big cookies gigantic cookies.

Is Simone's mother a pretty woman?

What Simone said is her mom has a bad case of sinus her nose drips but you won't notice in the dark. Her mom feels sorry for me I have to live here with you Dad without Mom so she asked me over for dinner but I told her I don't need Mom except to wash my socks that a mother after a while is a great pain and I'm just fine. Besides I have to take care of you which keeps me pretty busy are you sure you don't want to have an orgy?

I have to take a nap now Paul.

Are you dying Dad should I call the undertaker?

I'll feel better tomorrow Paul.

2

I'm right here Joe can you see me sitting here in the chair? Ah that made you sit up you devil you.

I hear you Goldie but I don't see you are you hiding in the closet?

Wish I was but I'm a ghost now Joe.

Oh no you didn't—

It was an accident just took one extra each time going closer and closer not really wanting to go over but oops I did so I'm gone now Joe all gone. Don't you feel sorry?

I'm so sorry Goldie I'll miss you it breaks my heart you were such a beauty.

I wish you could see me in this outfit made mostly out of old clouds how it shows off my legs they always caught your eye didn't they?

A married man Goldie which I was at the time doesn't look

at legs especially not a patient's but you had great legs and it's such a pity.

It feels so safe being dead nothing else terrible can happen it's a relief once in the shower I almost drowned which now I won't do but being dead has its drawbacks.

You're giving me Goldie a fantastic idea.

Your idea which I can read in your mind Joe if you don't mind me saying so stinks to high heaven.

We could have a great time together over there and I'd see your legs again so I'm coming over.

Let me give you some privileged information but you have to swear not to tell another living soul.

Okay I swear.

It's very boring on this side absolutely nothing to do we don't even have to cook which I used to hate but which now I'd give my right arm to rustle up a stack of flapjacks. Worst of all making out is definitely out and no dirty jokes and no beer and no cussing just all day the harps.

But I'm tired of everything life love work I've done it all and I'm exhausted and my wife's gone and now you're gone and what the hell'm I doing here?

The trouble with you Joe is you don't have any real misery to contend with daily hardships to keep your mind occupied something to strive for. Look at me I'd give anything to come back and be miserable.

You haven't heard Colleen's getting married bad enough she left I thought she still loved me anyway.

That woman with the mole on her behind?

Bertha.

Don't marry Bertha marry the one with the tiny nose.

May.

I can see into hearts now Joe and May makes up with her heart for what she lacks in a nose.

If I came over there Goldie we could float around on the clouds go to China New Zealand maybe even Siberia if we don't get shot down.

Only on earth you have clouds over here the sun shines every day without fail now that's boring out of your mind boring numbing.

I need to rest Goldie.

Well don't come over here to do it the music goes morning till night nonstop gives me a migraine then I have to stay up half the night to scare people.

Is that you Goldie the strange light in the chair?

It's me it is oh how simply wonderful I've never been a strange light before.

3

You're wearing on your head Joe my lace panties why?

You left them behind Colleen when you got down to brass tacks plain cotton.

Lace was for my frilly days Joe and I'm a woman of the world now and you look downright foolish sticking out the slits your floppy ears and pushing through the leg holes you have punk hair.

Watch out Joe she wants to get you back.

Goldie is that you?

Is something wrong dear who're you talking to?

Goldie is a ghost friend of mine Colleen.

I see Joe perhaps if you took them off your head you wouldn't hear strange voices.

Goldie's voice isn't strange it's an old favorite of mine Colleen.

But you look so foolish.

A pirate captain wears a hat like that the men are all with you Captain.

Thanks Paul.

First Mate Captain.

Thanks First Mate.

Should I hoist Mom up to the yardarm to swing for her life Captain?

I think not Paul but thanks just the same.

She doesn't deserve you anymore Joe after playing cutsie girl out there with the Biltmore man and who knows how many others?

We'll have Thanksgiving dinner Joe with the children and be a family again I'm over my foolishness and want my role as wife and mother back so my suitcases are in the hall and I'm all yours again Joe.

But will Joe forget his dick died the day you walked out tell her Joe she killed your dick and now maybe you don't want her back you want me.

What would I do with you?

What you always did with me.

Not you Colleen I mean Goldie are you listening Goldie what would I do with a strange light in my bed?

Dad I've come to say goodbye I've joined the CIA.

You're only 16 Paul.

You'll look good in dark glasses dear and I won't have to

watch you hobbling around with that foolish eyepatch when're you leaving dear?

Why do you encourage him Colleen for God's sake you're his mother he's a kid.

So he won't be around to string me up to the yardarm when I'm not looking so naturally I want him out of sight.

Paul the CIA doesn't employ boys it's against the law.

They said they can use my talents in covert actions but I don't know what covert means.

Sneaky dear the way you are if I had to raise you and your sister again I'd put you both on leashes to tie you up to pull you in to teach you to heel. Goodness you children were such spirited puppies.

I'll send you Dad the first ear I cut off but first I have to go to Virginia to learn to lie and steal for my country.

Don't be brave Paul it always gets you in the back of the neck and be sure to call.

I'll call if you accept the charges Dad bye Mom I really wouldn't hoist you up to the yardarm for more than five minutes.

I love you again in the same old way Joe maybe even more than ever now that I realize the great guy you are and what an idiot George is. In my dreams you kept calling to me to come back to fulfill all your desires so if you take the panties off your head you can get in the ones I have on if you know what I mean.

Don't listen to that Joe.

I have to admit Goldie it's a pretty good proposition.

Do you really see a ghost?

You see over there in that chair that light it's Goldie a former patient who ODeed so she's dead now.

You poor dear remembering a tragic life.

My unnatural cause of death—you and Colleen wouldn't know

this of course—requires me to live out my life as a ghost that's another 63 years so suppose I move in as your new wife?

With Colleen I have so many good memories and so many bad times we got through them all together I should take her back she makes great brownies too.

You were never crazy about my brownies dear.

Allergic to chocolate Colleen you know.

Frankly dear I always doubted that.

Choose me Joe I love you tons more.

Goldie I can't put my arms around you.

Smell my neck dear.

It's very sexy Colleen.

If I can find it in my soul to be sorry for my sins Joe are you listening—?

I am Goldie.

Take your nose out of there Joe.

Do I have to?

Dear don't listen to that ghost you'll drive yourself crazy.

—then I'll materialize into a woman again wouldn't that be exciting? Watch me now I'm feeling very repentant I feel it from the hair on my head down to my toes. You see me Joe am I materializing?

What's going on between you and that ghost?

I think you are Goldie this is every exciting look Colleen over there.

Oh God I was such a tramp broke men's hearts left and right hated my mother despised my sister told the most awful lies cheated the IRS loved you instead Joe. I'm sorry God please make me a good woman now so I can put on a little weight and not just be a strange light.

You're developing like a photograph Goldie I can see you.

Should I call a doctor dear mental health?

Look Colleen look.

I don't see a thing dear.

Goldie you're so beautiful you hardly have anything on.

You want to smell my neck too Joe it has a heavenly scent just take a whiff.

Would you mind Colleen if I smelled Goldie's neck?

I'm getting out of here dear call me when you don't see a ghost anymore you should take those panties off your head dear or someone might see you and call the police.

Goldie you're the girl of my dreams what color panties do you have on—gosh that's lovely.

MURDEROUS MYRTLE

After my wife, Gina, packed a bag and left, I found out that our bed is actually ten times bigger than I thought it was. Now I tell myself that Gina needed the space; she isn't petite. And when we slept together, I wasn't unhappy stretched out along one edge of the mattress like the mattress binding. In fact, I'm still stretched out along one edge of the mattress like the binding, while Gina is off somewhere in pursuit of adventure. In our bed now her big space remains unoccupied. She's been gone for three months and I'm glad for her. The only worry I have is that she might come home and get back in bed again.

At this moment it's possibly Gina unlocking the back door. It wakes me in bed with a fright. The locks, it occurred to me when she left, should have been changed. But changed locks wouldn't stop Gina if she wanted to come inside. And to replace the door she'd break down to come inside would be costly, so I left the locks unchanged.

But it isn't Gina coming in the back door. It's Myrtle Feinberg with ice in her blue eyes and a fresh razor blade between her teeth. I suppose that Myrtle does not want me to miss the fact that she has in her possession a razor blade, and so has positioned it between her teeth to draw my undivided attention. Fine, it draws my undivided attention. But it doesn't impress me. A curved, two-edged sword between her teeth, now that would impress me, not an ordinary Gillette single-edged blade. It's too early for me to get up and shave.

"The alarm hasn't gone off yet."

"When," Myrtle mumbles, then removes the blade from her teeth so she can speak clearly, "when I got up this morning, Richard Farnsworth, I immediately wanted to get my hands on something sharp." She sits down on the foot of the bed and holds the blade over her left wrist—the one with the diamond watch. "But I was in a hurry to get here," she says, "so I picked up this blade of yours, instead of one of Alex's."

I gave Myrtle a key to the back door weeks ago because she thinks I might die from heartbreak over Gina's departure. Myrtle wants to find my dead body before the silverfish and cockroaches in the house find it. She's determined to help me recover from Gina's absence, even though it was Gina's presence that was making me sick, and from which, now that she's gone, I'm slowly recovering. And Myrtle, in return, wants help in remembering what it was she and Alex used to do in bed together.

For nine years Myrtle has been married to Alex. In the last two years, however, they forgot what it was they used to do in bed. Every marriage, Myrtle says, breaks down one way or another every seven years, hers with Alex, mine with Gina. But while Myrtle still sticks with Alex, she doesn't know why. To do what? It drives Myrtle crazy trying to remember what they used to do. In the hope that I can jog her memory, she hangs around with me. But, frankly, I don't remember myself what Gina and I used to do. And Myrtle's husband, Alex, is no help either.

Alex, for the last two years, has been taking one little pill in the morning, another at night, so he sleeps like a baby, and stays tranquil all day. He used to be a fanatic athlete, a fanatic mathematician, a wild man, Myrtle says, who used to make her wild too. But now they're both so tranquil, Alex from the pills, and Myrtle because she sleeps with a six-foot pill.

When Myrtle found me lying out at the beach weeks ago, she said I looked devastated by Gina's departure, despite the lovely ladies in my company, tourists up for the weekend from Hollywood. In swimsuits not much bigger than pasties, the lovely ladies said they were looking for a good time. So I asked them geography questions and math problems, and their answers kept us in stitches even though I didn't know the right answers myself. It was the most I could do, besides look at them, although I was sure there was something else I should have been doing. For a reason which I couldn't fathom, it pleased me a lot to look at them in their pseudo pasties.

"Someday," Myrtle says to me, "we'll both figure out what to do in bed."

Myrtle and I are stockbrokers at the same Hutton office here in town. But I, with Gina gone, now often take off from work to lie out on East Beach where Dan Rather and friends used to lie out themselves when that guy, what's-his-name, came to town. Myrtle, when she found me at the beach that day, had also intended to lie out, but instead zeroed in on me. After she sent my lovely ladies packing, Myrtle dragged me back to my own house. And to my amazement, in my kitchen, without using any chicken, because my freezer was bare, Myrtle cooked up some delicious chicken soup just for me.

But the next day I caught the worst flu of my life. I'm sure the soup didn't *cause* the flu, but it is an interesting speculation to think about. Anyway, Myrtle, for the last three weeks, has been coming over to my house without, of course, Alex's knowledge, and she says she'll help me to get well, and together we'll figure out the true purpose for which the bed was invented.

"I know," I said yesterday, "the bed was invented for sick people."

Now, Myrtle, at the foot of the bed says, "Richard Farnsworth—" She always says both my names as if I might have forgotten which Richard I am. "I want to cut something." She gazes at me, but I play dumb. "Do you hear me?" she says.

I decide to nod my head to prevent her from performing surgery on my ears with the razor blade.

"I'm desperate to cut something," she says a little louder.

"In the fridge," I finally say, "there's half a liverwurst, Myrtle. Go cut yourself a slice of liverwurst."

"It's myself I want to cut," Myrtle says. "I want to bleed to death in this new silk dress, which I bought just for you, with this sweetheart neckline. Do you like it?" The razor blade is now held over her left wrist again.

If I don't like the dress, does she intend to slash her wrists? Is this some new technique to jog our memories? Is the razor blade like the primal scream used to be? The dress is very pretty, however, and I like it, so she's safe this time.

"It's the sexiest thing," I say, "that I've ever seen you in."

"Do you know why I want to cut my wrists?" she says. "It really has nothing to do with the dress. I just told you about the dress because I want to be a good-looking corpse for morgue attendants. No one who commits suicide ever thinks of morgue attendants who have to put up with bloated drowned victims slimy from the ocean." It seems Myrtle isn't kidding. One point of the blade touches her skin. "Watch me," she fumes, "you heartless bastard."

When a tiny speck of blood appears on her wrist, I lunge for the razor blade and we wrestle, and I think that suicide can be fun. She holds on to the blade as I force it away from her skin. About a half hour later, in the melee, her dress comes off, and underneath, she's stark naked. I have no idea what to do with a naked woman in my bed, except to cover her with a blanket so she won't catch the flu. But Myrtle examines various features of her figure and seems puzzled as to why they are there. Then we decide, for the time being, to sleep on it.

When we wake up around noon, she explains that a mutual friend of ours has the previous evening seen me in a restaurant with a gorgeous redhead. Jealousy has driven Myrtle to despair and thoughts of suicide.

"If you ever see her again," Myrtle says, "I'll kill myself for sure, and my death will be on your conscience."

No woman has ever before offered to kill herself over me, so it seems like a nice compliment, but to cut her wrists in my bed, to soak my mattress with her eight quarts of blood, seems a trifle spiteful too. Now we both get dressed and go to Hutton to hustle customers into buying shares so we can earn our commissions.

What interests me about Myrtle is that she wants to restore

my mind when, personally, I think it's never been in such good shape before. Friends of mine no longer will pull a chair out from under me, or if I drop my car keys kick me, or if I walk in the neighborhood call the police. My friends, when my wife Gina was still at home, had just tried to instill in me the spark of life, but I was then a hopeless case, which shamelessly I rather enjoyed a little too. Last night, even though I didn't know what else to do with her, I went to dinner with the redhead, and tonight I'm going to dinner with her again, and I think I'm getting warm. Just looking at the redhead something seems to happen to me. I seem to swell up a bit.

The next morning Myrtle arrives with a scratch already drawn across her left wrist. Between her teeth again she has another fresh blade of mine. She's using up, damn it, all my new blades. "I followed you myself last night," she says. "And you went out with the redhead again. So now, I'm going to do it right here, spill my blood all over your sheets."

"Please don't," I plead. "Since Gina left, I haven't figured out yet how to use the washing machine. In the guest room there's three months of dirty clothes and dirty sheets piled up."

"Did you get into the redhead's pants?" Myrtle screams. A little light goes on in her eyes, as if she has just revealed to herself, by accident, a forgotten fact. But she sobers up and adds, "I'm going to die now, Richard Farnsworth, unless, unless . . ."

"Unless what?" I say. "What? Try to remember."

"It has something to do with my pants," she says, "which I don't have on."

"Maybe if you wore your pants under your dress," I say, "we'd figure out our problem."

"We'll never figure it out," Myrtle whines. "And besides, I'm jealous of your redhead. So the solution for me is suicide."

Again I leap for the razor blade and again we wrestle. Minutes later I have the blade and I throw it out of reach. The scratch on her wrist is minor and I kiss it. In time, I'm sure, our minds will clear and as mature adults we, too, will commit adultery, which seems in the cards for us, whatever adultery is. I look it up in the dictionary, which defines it as illicit sexual relations. But what are sexual relations? It's something that Myrtle and I, and for that matter, Alex, too, have to figure out, and fast, before we die and can't get any more.

The redhead, of course, says she knows all about sexual relations, and will explain it all to me in her condo, for a modest fee. She's a therapist, and all I have to do is sign a contract for forty-eight years of hourly sessions and all my troubles will be over.

"How about it?" she says, the next evening at dinner, when she unfolds the contract on the table.

"I'll sign up," I say, "just as soon as I put some ink in my fountain pen." It's my ruse to get out of there, and fast, at the end of our third dinner date.

This time Myrtle herself is waiting outside the restaurant with another razor blade in her teeth. But I have on my new suit from Hong Kong which would wrinkle in another wrestling match, so I steer clear of physical contact with Myrtle.

"Look," I say to her, "I'm tired of this suicide business. If you have to do it, you just have to do it—and I'm sorry. So just go ahead and do it, and get it over with, slash your wrists, slash your throat, see if I care."

"You heartless bastard you," she says. "You'd let me kill myself?"

"If you have your mind made up," I say. "But first, tell me, did you decide for cremation or burial? I can let Alex know what to do with your remains."

"Don't you, Richard Farnsworth, have any pity in your heart? Am I killing myself over a Neanderthal?" A sob escapes from her throat. "Are you an insensitive homo erectus? Is that what the secret love of my life turns out to be?"

"I'm afraid so," I say. "It's such a pain in the ass to be sensitive. My dad was sensitive, and he had to drink himself to death. So I've decided to be completely indifferent to pain and suffering everywhere. It feels just great."

"Your life isn't worth living," she sneers as other diners coming out of the restaurant, or heading in, stop to listen and circle around us. "I'm the sensitive one," Myrtle says. "I stop to smell the flowers." A sudden blush of happiness is in her face. "So I won't slit my wrists; my own life is worth living. I'll slit, instead, your wrists, Richard Farnsworth." Then Myrtle comes at me with my own razor blade raised like an ax about to separate my hands from my forearms.

But the crowd parts in the nick of time and Alex appears striding to us in the center; and he snatches Myrtle up in his arms. "I was worried, Myrtle, that you were seeing another man," he says. "So I followed you." He squeezes her in his arms. She goes limp and drops the razor blade. "When my dealer was busted," he says, "I ran out of little pills. Then I remembered what the bed is for."

"What's it for?" Myrtle weakly says.

"It's for sexual relations," Alex says.

"And what's that?" she sighs.

"It's leapfrog and tick-tack-toe combined," he says. And the crowd applauds. "We're going home to our bed," he says.

And I, too, go home to my own bed, and there under the covers is Gina. Her Marine Corps uniform is scattered on the floor around the bed. She says, "I enlisted, Richard, but then I missed you so much, so I came back." From under the covers her arms come out and reach for me. They look like the arms of an orangutan.

"Won't you," I say, "be thrown into the stockade for going AWOL?"

"Only if the MPs find out where I am," she says. "And I won't tell them. And you won't tell them either, right, dear?"

"Right, dear," I say.

CAKES

That summer he sweated first from the humidity which in 1940 everyone in Brooklyn sweated from; then he sweated from the hot ovens at Carlo Amato's pastry shop in Bensonhurst four or five nights a week; then he sweated from the hot ovens at a pastry shop downtown every day of the week except on Sunday, when he usually slept until noon. From downtown, Giovanni Vitale came home at the end of a workday on the BMT subway to his wife, Lisa, to their three kids, Anna, Steve, and Johnny. After dinner they would all listen to the Philco. Then Giovanni and the eldest kid, Johnny, eleven, walked three long blocks and two short blocks, past the old people who fanned themselves on the stoops, to Carlo's shop on Seventeenth Avenue.

For five dollars extra, that August night's work began with a batch of cannoli. The burned lard once again was ladled from a tall can into a large copper pot which was put on the ring stove with its lone, very big and very hot burner. When the cannoli wrapped on short broomsticks were fried to a crisp, they bobbed up to the surface of the steamy and boiling lard and he scooped them out with a strainer.

"You want some coffee I could give you, or a sandwich?" the shop owner's wife, Martina Amato, asked Giovanni. "How about you, Johnny? You want some ice cream, some soda?" Johnny watched his father as his father watched the woman get the coffee. Carlo Amato, who usually baked the goods sold in his own shop, had nodded from a small marble table without moving from his chair when Giovanni and Johnny came in. Giovanni had nodded back. Carlo wasn't too strong, Giovanni had said to his son, so he helped Carlo out at night, as Johnny helped him out. With Johnny's help, father and son would finish up by eleven instead of after midnight for the father alone. The next morning Johnny would still be sleepy, and his mother would tickle his toes until he climbed out of bed for breakfast with his sister and brother. By then his father would already be on the subway headed again for the pastry shop downtown.

"Hey, Dad, in the flour here, moving around, are some brown things, you ought to see this." Johnny was at the mixer where he put in a scoop of flour after his previous scoop was worked in by the blade that rotated. "I put in two scoops, but you ought to see this, Dad. I don't think I should put in any more. I see what they are. Bugs. The flour is crawling with bugs. Wow! Look at those bugs."

A Chesterfield was attached to Giovanni's lower lip when he came over with his hands covered with tufts of yellow butter cream which he whipped by hand in another copper pot and his cigarette would be ruined if he touched it. "In the flour after a while the eggs hatch," he said. "Insects lay them in the wheat in the field. When we bake the cookies, it won't matter; the bugs will melt. In some countries, they eat things like ants and grasshoppers." The movement of his lip as he spoke caused the long ash at the end of his cigarette to drop into the dough with the insects. Johnny reached in for the ash but he was quickly yanked back by his father. "Never, never do that." The risky things a son could do worried him even though Giovanni was too tired to worry about bugs and cigarette ash in the dough. After Johnny hesitated a moment over his father's easy acceptance of the bugs, he too decided that it was no big deal. Even the cigarette ash in the dough that turned with the blade was forgotten after Johnny covered the ash with another scoop of flour.

Back at the marble-top worktable big enough for two pastrymen, Giovanni would make next a batch of *sfudelle.* Ghostly white, his face and arms covered with flour, he rolled out a sheet of dough until it was thin as cloth and then rolled it up like a thick window shade. With a broad blade, he sliced it like bread, and using his quick and calloused fingers, he then fanned out the slices until half the rings were on top and half were on bottom. Between the dough-hinged halves, he stuffed the yellow butter cream.

The physical work, the heat from the ovens with their wide mouths and black iron doors one above the other in two rows from about the level of his knees to above his head, the long hours for little pay in those times when most other Sicilians too didn't earn enough to buy many cakes—when almost no one was well off—all these conditions left Giovanni little time for anything else but more work; maybe one joke for his own kids, maybe two tender words for Lisa. To keep doing his work, he found pleasure from the batches that looked good and tasted good with nothing wasted or burned or flushed down the toilet where a failed batch was sent. Another pleasure he had was when he told stories about his bachelor days when he ice-skated in Central Park with the rich girls who lived in brownstones off Fifth Avenue nearby and how they brought him presents and behind the bushes he kissed them—but they wouldn't take him home.

"I don't believe you, Giovanni, that you kissed so many girls that you said you kissed," said Martina, at the small table with her husband where they both sipped black coffee with anisette. Her husband's face turned to her and then to Giovanni, but Carlo really looked elsewhere, inside himself or out past the shop to a distant place. Giovanni understood, but there was nothing he could do for Carlo, aside from the cakes he made for his old friend. Martina said, "You should go to bed now, Carlo. It's better you don't stay up so late. I close up the shop myself."

"I'm not so tired," Carlo said. "About Giovanni, for myself, I believe him. I believe he kissed all the girls he said, because he gave them his *biscotti,* from the recipe from his father. Not because he is so handsome. Tell me, who is more handsome, me or Giovanni?"

"You are more handsome, Carlo," his wife said, as she touched his wavy white hair.

"He is," agreed Giovanni. "He still has all his hair while mine is half gone."

Into the center of stars and half-moons that would be baked

as cookies, Johnny pressed pieces of red or green maraschino cherries. He looked over at his father and then looked at Carlo and thought that his father was more handsome. There was no doubt about it. When Johnny had placed the cookies in the pans, his father shuffled the pans like oversized playing cards into the ovens. The anise biscuits that his father had just taken out of the ovens Johnny carried to the front shop, where he would stack them up. While out there he also had a slice of spumoni and soda-jerked a soda for himself that was mostly chocolate syrup. At that late hour no customers had come into the front shop, which had white walls and white floor tiles and white fluorescents. All that white helped Johnny to keep his eyes open.

Quietly the boy sat behind the counter and worked there, and when Carlo later came by and suggested that Johnny also sample the tortoni which were in the freezer, Johnny took a tortoni too. Carlo went out the door and up to the apartment over the shop. In the ceiling Johnny could hear Carlo's footsteps and wondered if Carlo would be all right. Then he went to the back shop to ask his father if he would like to have a tortoni.

With the ricotta cream, his father stuffed the fresh cannoli skins he had just made. At the small table with her forehead on her arm, Martina cried softly to herself: at this late hour she could no longer pretend that Carlo's illness was just a bad dream; if she could drain her tears, then she too could go upstairs and hold Carlo as if her arms could keep him here.

"Sure, bring me a tortoni, please," his father said. "And bring me a glass of soda water, plain."

Then Johnny carried the pans of baked stars and half-moons out to the front shop, where he dusted them with a large shaker of powdered sugar, and also now and then dusted his own tongue. Between yawns, he built the cookies up in trays decorated with doilies. To stay awake he tried to think about the Harley he intended to have someday, but when he put his head down for two seconds, he dropped off. The old couple who came in minutes later for lemon ice startled him. He went to get Martina, who came out to serve them, and after they left she stayed there while Johnny tried again to build up the cookies. His head nodded more than once and he had to jerk himself awake. So Martina seated herself beside him, put her arms around him, and before he knew what happened his eyes closed and his face went down on her breast where he was held like that. For half an hour he slept there until his father finished up and came out to the front shop, where he half-filled a sack with cookies and biscuits to take home to the family.

"You have to wake up now," Giovanni said as he shook the boy.

As his eyes snapped open, Johnny said, "I'm wide awake."

INSIDE THE FIRE

Where the elevated line over New Urecht Avenue curved into the airspace over Sixteenth Avenue the three- and four-storied walk-ups on both sides were so close to the train tracks that even the arc light of this August morning couldn't reach Sergio and the others who lived on the sidewalks below. The shops there were also nearly in constant darkness with customers who came in only to look for a bargain or if shops on other streets had closed up for the day.

Besides a lack of light there was also a lack of quiet on the avenue. The noise day and night of train wheels grinding by sounded like prison doors to some of the guys who now lived on the sidewalks. Some of the longtimers had become a little deaf from the train noise and those guys whenever they had something to say would shout it, even if at that moment no train passed by to shout over. In that way too, and with his hands cupped at his mouth for a megaphone besides, Sergio Rinaldo shouted this morning to his friend Giancarlo that he would give Becky a party tomorrow on her fortieth birthday. She had told him and others about it over the past few weeks. While Sergio pondered where and how to get the party fixings, Giancarlo should go around to invite the others. Up and down the avenue then Giancarlo shouted the invitation to lots of homeless guys and to the few homeless women, and some shouted back that they would come to the party.

"Eight guys and two dames said they'd come," said Giancarlo that night in Sergio's cellar. "You want their names, Sergio?"

"I don't want their names, Giancarlo. Anyone's welcome to come to the party. Maybe the people at the party could also be an audience to hear my jokes. I've been writing some new jokes."

"Please, don't tell no jokes, Sergio. You ain't funny no more," said Giancarlo. "Neither is sleeping down here funny which you think it is. This place is a rat hole, Sergio."

"A cellar has its drawbacks, Giancarlo. But look where you sleep, in a hallway, when two guys in hallways already got killed by persons unknown," said Sergio. He grinned over the candle as they both squatted on the floor. From his years in the comedy business he knew that candlelight under the chin distorted the face with shadows, but his ghoulish expression didn't make Giancarlo laugh. "Let me show you what the terrier caught that I hung up to dry," said Sergio, who liked to see people react, preferably with a belly laugh, in order for them and him to know they were all still alive. He lit another squat candle—he had taken a full box from the candle rack before the Sacred Heart Shrine at Saint Finbar's. In the light of the second candle he lured Giancarlo to the back of the cellar despite the stink and Giancarlo's better judgment. Giancarlo was curious. Along the back wall Giancarlo saw the dead rats hung heads down with their tails knotted on a length of clothesline and he felt queasy.

"You're pretty weird," said Giancarlo, who hunched back toward the other candle, which still flickered on the floor. In the dark he stepped on the dog's tail. "Sorry, Pagliaccio," he said to the dog. "Go back to sleep, Pagliaccio."

"A rat ain't stupid," said Sergio, when he too squatted by the candle on the floor again. "When it sees its buddies hung there, it will scoot out of this cellar while a guy and his dog try to get some sleep."

"I came here tonight to talk about Becky," said Giancarlo, getting down to business. "Becky ain't so sure she wants to come to her own party in the same old dress she's had on for months now, Sergio." Giancarlo's small body twitched as his eyes failed to poke holes in the cellar darkness all around him as he sat close to the candle. "She said if you're such a great guy, Sergio, who gives a lady a birthday party, then you can also give her the dress to come in. And she needs shoes too. I would know what kind of shoes to get her if you want to." Giancarlo Gargano had been one of five shoe salesmen in a store on 86th Street there in Bensonhurst when his wife, Cynthia, decided that he wouldn't ever earn enough money for the family to live decently on so she had moved herself and their two kids in with the owner of the store. After the store owner fired Giancarlo, he couldn't pay his rent and lost the apartment besides and then decided there wasn't anyone to work for anyway, not even for himself, a poor specimen of a man if he had ever seen one. So without a job or savings or an apartment he moved onto the avenue. "You're not going to believe this, Sergio: Becky said what she wants for a present for her birthday—are you listening?—besides the dress and the shoes, is for you to *marry* her, Sergio. Do you believe that? If I was you, Sergio, I wouldn't marry her. On account of I think she has a case of crabs."

"That's an awful lot for a woman to ask a guy for, Giancarlo, for a birthday present. But. I just might do it. I had a lot of women in my time, but I never married one, which maybe wasn't so nice of me. Now I'm forty-four maybe it's time," said Sergio, who was considered by women to be good-looking despite his long needle nose, because of the way his eyes and mouth twinkled, as they now did. A few people would come to a birthday party but many more would come to a wedding, he thought, so he would have a bigger audience for his jokes too. He was hungry for an audience after going a couple of years without one, but he still called his former agent on Seventh Avenue in Manhattan, who always told a performer up front how bad he was but never how good he was when he was good. For years Sergio had been very good. The customers had rolled in the aisles. But then Sergio was told on the phone twenty or so times that his light touch had turned into hot lead, and the agent couldn't book him anywhere. Sergio kept his show clothes on under his ragged clothes, though, for when he would go on again, and he called his former agent whenever he had some extra change, which wasn't often. His slightly bonkers form of humor had taken the funnyman over the edge, the agent had decided, so he humored Sergio. "There's a gig up in the Catskills I turned down for you for the lousy money they offered which couldn't hardly cover what they charge for lox and bagels, but another deal that my fingers are crossed about could be your breakthrough shot, Sergio, so call me again in a few weeks." A call like that could give Sergio enough adrenaline to go for a few days without even the thought of food as hope seeped down from his ears into his flesh as far down as his toes, which even he couldn't stand the smell of. He didn't take his shoes off now, even when he slept in the wire basket which once had been a city trash container. The wire basket had first been co-opted by some Sicilian in the neighborhood for his personal use as a backyard incinerator, and then it was discarded when some wires had burned through and co-opted this last time by Sergio for him to sleep in in the cellar under the shoe repair shop. In the summer now the shoe repairman didn't come down to the cellar to check on the oil burner, and when he went home to his own apartment on 80th Street at the end of the day Sergio went down into the cellar. Before the shoe repairman came back to work in the morning, Sergio would already be gone for breakfast for himself and his dog, Pagliaccio. Sergio thought the terrier had the sad heart of a clown and for that reason named him Clown in Italian, the language Sergio had grown up with and which belonged to the neighborhood. He used Italian as much as his native English now that he was back in Bensonhurst.

"If this is one of your jokes, I'm not playing it on Becky, because she won't laugh at no joke, Sergio. She ain't in her right mind to laugh at anything," said Giancarlo. "If she could be cleaned up with some turpentine like once my Cynthia used to get out the nits from my daughter Angelina's hair, then Becky could look all right and then maybe her mind would come back in one piece."

"After we get married Becky could come down here in the cellar too to sleep at night," said Sergio, his plan for their future as solid proof of his serious intention, that he wasn't just kidding, though often he *was* just kidding. "I even know where there's another wire basket for her to sleep in." He had to laugh out loud right then even though Giancarlo didn't see the joke. Sergio visualized himself and Becky sleeping side by side in wire baskets in the cellar, and he knew that was funny and crazy. But also it wasn't so funny and crazy either, because they wouldn't have any other home to sleep in.

The audience in the nightclub where he had last worked also hadn't laughed when he made up a story about a homeless guy who gave a birthday party for a bag lady, and now he himself was going to be a character in that story except that it wasn't fiction anymore. The audience should have laughed—he had insisted to the nightclub owner—instead of booing him. Boos wouldn't help anyone to feel better the way a few laughs would. Canned from his last club date, he stayed in the fleabag hotel on West 47th Street in the room he shared with Corinne, who worked at the same club as a waitress. She wore a tutu to show off in black net stockings the Statue of Liberty long legs he thought she had. Legs which also drove some guys crazy. Corinne kept Sergio around to beat off those crazy guys, but she and Sergio both knew that they were just temporary shelter for each other like the room they had. Nothing was expected or given except a little kindness, a little company, and a roll in the hay. "Personally, Sergio, I think you're the funniest palooka I ever heard in my life, but myself, I don't think no audience wants to hear the awful truth," said Corinne. "What it wants to hear out on a date and having drinks is good news only. Do yourself a favor, pal, go take yourself out of the funny routines. Go get yourself a regular job."

All his life the few people who had really liked him had urged on him grown-up behavior while the others who hadn't liked him had left him alone to be a kid, which was the only work he had ever succeeded at. As a teenager he had been foolish and devilish and dangerous without hurting anyone else, a borderline delinquent, but he had no malice, not that his heart was overflowing with the milk of human kindness. Any kid's heart was more or less empty of feelings for others until it could get enough feelings stored away for the kid himself, and Sergio too was still trying to store away feelings for himself. Not only did he get in trouble because of the kid he was, but the kid he was also got him out of trouble when an adult in his shoes would have drawn a blank on what to do next.

For a few months Corinne covered their expenses, but she couldn't convince Sergio to take a job as a short-order cook in a Broadway burger joint or to unload building materials for a new office tower going up on Third Avenue. Corinne had arranged this job through the foreman she was seeing on the side in the process of letting go of Sergio and having someone ready to take his place. When all the signs were clear to Sergio that Corinne wouldn't boot him out but that he wasn't wanted anymore either, he left on his own and went back to Bensonhurst. His widowed mother still lived there, but he wouldn't go to see her until her last days when she would be too sick to tell him what to do.

Seated across from Sergio in the cellar, Giancarlo wrapped his arms around his shoulders to protect himself from Sergio, the madman, who laughed for no reason it seemed, and to protect himself too from the darkness down there, and the rats. "You can't get married to Becky tomorrow without a license and a priest," said Giancarlo. "It takes weeks to get a license and a priest, and besides, we don't have any money to get them. And where, I ask you, are you going to get a dress and shoes from by tomorrow?"

"A license and a priest in order to get married is bullshit, Giancarlo. Let's dispense with the bullshit, especially us in our circumstances. What we have to deal with here, Giancarlo, is two warm bodies to be joined in the married state, Becky because she wants to, and me because I been asked. But do you know what—I'm getting this strange thought in my mind, the way a woman sometimes knows what you're thinking before you do, that I'm the wrong guy she asked. That she should've asked you, Giancarlo. That you're the guy who really wants to marry her. You really go for Becky, don't you, Giancarlo?"

"Me?" said Giancarlo. "No, I don't go for Becky. I think she's nice. I think she was once a beauty. But she's a little wacky, Sergio. Besides, my wife, Cynthia, didn't divorce me yet, on account of it's against the rules of the church. It don't bother her it's against the rules to sleep with that guy. If I married Becky it would be bigamy. I could go to jail for bigamy, Sergio."

"First, Giancarlo, there ain't no bigamy where we are on Sixteenth Avenue," said Sergio. "Second, if *I* married Becky, I would just be doing her a favor, which is the only thing left I can do anymore. But *you* really care about her. That's very touching, Giancarlo. You two could take over this here cellar. I'd move out to your hallway."

"She asked to marry you," said Giancarlo. "She didn't ask to marry me." His hands covered his face to hide the disappointment he had had since he was a kid when the daily routines had already begun to seem too difficult to manage. "In the first place,

I didn't have no grand idea like you did to give her a birthday party, Sergio."

"It's settled, Giancarlo. You ask her, and I'm sure she'll say yes," said Sergio. "And I'm going to be the priest myself. And I'm going to prepare the wedding feast too. It'll be a birthday party *and* a wedding feast. So, go ask her, Giancarlo. I'm sure it's you Becky wanted to ask all along, but maybe she thought you were too good for her, which I wouldn't be as a lunatic former funnyman."

"What about the dress and shoes, Sergio? If I believed you'd get them and I could bring her the good news, then maybe she wouldn't mind marrying me instead," said Giancarlo. "But you can't get no dress and no shoes, can you?"

"Yes, I can. I'll tell you how, Giancarlo. I'm going to force my way in where your first wife, Cynthia, lives now by showing her my knife. You know it's a genuine hunting knife," said Sergio. "I'm going to ask her very politely for the favorite dress you used to like to see her in. And she's going to give it to me."

"You'll scare my kids," said Giancarlo.

"When they come out, then I'll go in," said Sergio. "I promise you I won't scare them. Now tell me which dress I should ask for."

"The ivory satin one with a few pearls sewed on up here," said Giancarlo. "But don't hurt her, Sergio. I still love her, Sergio."

"I know you do, Giancarlo. So I'll be very nice. And she'll be very nice and give me the dress," said Sergio. But it was all a joke for the pleasure of revenge it seemed to give Giancarlo on his wife, and also to urge Giancarlo forward into marriage with Becky. Sergio saw himself now with a thin Machiavellian heart, but he had no remorse. A comedian by nature had to be a certified bastard, in his opinion, which made it possible for him to attack the bad guys. The sweet guys like Giancarlo just didn't have the heart to do it.

Footsteps overhead woke him the next morning in the cellar, where he had overslept huddled down at the bottom of the wire basket like a week's accumulated trash, but he was pleased when he opened his eyes that in his sleep his mind had figured out the menu for that night's wedding feast. Promptly he pushed himself up and out of the basket. He said to Pagliaccio that they didn't have time for their usual piss on the back wall to warn the rats not to live in their cellar, but Sergio smelled in the humidity the dog's product. The dog hadn't been able to hold himself. It was a quality a dog was expected to have but not one that had to sleep in a vermin-infested cellar and whose previous owner had arranged for its vocal cords to be surgically cut. Only now had this dog ever been praised for its natural terrier talent as a born ratter. A year ago Sergio had made a dollar deposit at the pound, and for three days he had panhandled on 86th Street until he had enough money to pay the fee for the dog. But no money had been left over for a collar and a leash, and Sergio knew now that Pagliaccio at least deserved a better life than he was able to give him, including a better collar and leash than a length of clothesline, which he now tied to the dog's neck. Without a bark from Pagliaccio they then left the cellar, both on soft paws.

If the dollar in change in his pocket that he had panhandled the day before was enough to buy a thrift-store dress he would give up his and Pagliaccio's breakfast this morning, but more than a dollar was needed—inspiration was needed, and there was no inspiration without coffee first. When the pimple-faced counter kid bagged the coffee and doughnuts, Sergio asked him for ten creams and ten sugars instead of the usual eight. For a moment the kid squinted and seemed poised with an obscenity on the tip of his tongue but instead bagged more creams and sugars than Sergio could count and handed the bag over without a word or a grin. Seated on the curb under the elevated where the darkness and noise comforted him like a blanket he was hiding under with the radio on, he read a discarded copy of this morning's *Daily News*, and with the exception of the coffee, which he kept for himself, he shared the doughnuts, creams, and sugars with Pagliaccio. The dog had a brown tattered coat of short hair but only half a tail, which never wagged. He looked like a joke on all fours, but often Sergio fed him when he himself would go unfed. Not even a square meal made the tail wag, though. Sergio did all the talking, commented on world events, and not even once did Pagliaccio bark back, and when Sergio told his dog a funny story as he did every morning to keep in shape for the time he returned as a top banana, the dog without vocal cords couldn't laugh either. He was a hopeless case.

Inspired by the coffee now, Sergio left Sixteenth Avenue with Pagliaccio on the clothesline leash and they made their way back to 79th Street, which was a few streets away. He was now unrecognized there by the other kids from his time who had stayed on the street to become adults like their parents and who eyed him suspiciously though once they had been close friends. He and the dog went down the block to the house where he himself had lived and where his mother still lived. After he looked around for a self-appointed spy on his actions, he shrunk to half his size as he crawled under the alley windows to the backyard clothesline where as a high school sophomore he had stolen the upstairs girl's underpants. But at this early hour of the morning there were no drying clothes to be stolen for Becky to wear, so he had to beat a hasty retreat.

His next stop was St. Finbar's sacristy, where he went in, noticed by a young priest who was putting on his cassock to go to offer the sacrifice of the mass in a few minutes, but the priest also *un*noticed Sergio by turning his back on the handout Sergio was expected to ask for. When the priest was gone Sergio helped himself to another priestly garment from a wood peg where the clothes were hung. It looked like a white dress which was usually worn over the black cassock. In this instance the white garment also had a very wide lace border at the bottom which triggered in Sergio's memory a terrifically funny story he used to tell about a priest in lace, and right there in the sacristy he laughed out loud at his own remembered punch line. Then he was out the door with the dresslike surplice when an old woman all in black coming toward him spotted the garment and screamed, "Crook! Crook!" He dropped the priestly dress at her feet, which didn't quiet her, so he hotfooted it away from there.

At the Salvation Army store where he went next the clerk gave him a dress at no charge, as simple as that, when he said he had no money to buy one for a bride-to-be. In order to receive the dress he also had to accept a pamphlet about how to save his soul, which seemed very funny to him when he couldn't even save his ass. The dress wasn't ivory satin with pearls but it was pretty close as a sort of yellowed white cotton and it was clean. It was also a bit too spacious, as apparently it had been cast off by some well-fed woman while Becky herself was all bones, but the size wouldn't matter. "If you'd let me tell you a funny story it would be my way of paying you for the dress," Sergio said to the clerk, who was a glum old man with fallen shoulders. The man said, "I don't have time to laugh. I have to wait on the other customers." He put the dress into a brown sack printed with a supermarket's name. Then Sergio untied the dog from the bike rack by the front door and together they went to find Becky.

To lengthen his own pleasure in the preparation of the feast Sergio had struck a match early, using the trash on the avenue and in the empty lots for his fire, and even some from his cellar. The fire had burned for hours now in the wire trash basket, since Giancarlo said he wouldn't want the basket to sleep in with Becky if they moved into the cellar, and Sergio knew the basket wouldn't fit in the hallway where he would move to. Giancarlo said that he and Becky would sleep in sleeping bags in the cellar.

Meat couldn't be barbecued successfully over roaring flames, Sergio knew from his better days. Flames would just scorch the meat but the radiant heat of hot coals would penetrate the meat so it would cook inside too, so he had built up a bed of hot coals. The smell of the meat that roasted on the coals traveled under the elevated to the figures in doorways, sprawled on sidewalks, and huddled in the empty lots. Some of the ragged men and women were so lost in their own nightmares that they had already forgotten that they had been invited to the birthday and wedding party. But their noses reminded them now and they pulled themselves up as if real life called to them once again. They sniffed the night air like animals for the direction the smell was coming from. Starved so often, many had given up even the appetite for food as earlier they had given up the appetites for sex, comfort, and the simple pleasures that sustained normal lives. Still, now, from many small caves in the grand cave under the elevated the figures shuffled unsurely like ghosts in the night toward the red glow in the basket as the memory of what a feast could be came back to them.

Of the two women in the crowd of men, one was the plumpest of them all and had her wits about her to rent a post office box where she received checks which she deposited at a bank and withdrew a few dollars each weekday for food. Some days she also took out a little money to buy a little gas to move the car she slept in when a notice was posted on the windshield that warned if the car wasn't moved in seventy-two-hours it would be towed away. The car's right side was crushed in like a tin can under a heel, but she had bought the car that way from a junk dealer for a hundred dollars to have a place to sleep with locked doors and to get out of the snow in winter. The other woman guest had none of her wits about her at all, evident in the endless loud conversations she had with a man apparently dead before she could tell him everything on her mind. Her speech was in fragments that gaped with holes where the meaning should be and no one had the least idea what she was saying.

Now, close to midnight, a third woman came up the middle of the avenue. It was Becky in the yellowed white cotton dress, holding on to Giancarlo's arm as both took measured steps in time with an organ playing in their minds as they approached the altar and the ceremony. Their path was lighted by twin young men of low intellect who struck and held burning paper matches until their fingers almost caught fire. They then moved a few paces ahead in the summer night to strike more matches for the bride and groom. The avenue was deserted by the other people who had beds to go to, and, as Sergio had anticipated, quite a big crowd of his and Giancarlo's friends had turned out for the party, a much larger crowd than for a birthday alone.

The nuptial couple and all the guests came to stand in a stretched-out circle around the basket cooker in which the main course rested on the hot coals themselves, as Sergio hadn't been able to locate a roasting grate. With a pair of charred wood sticks Sergio turned the roast for it to cook evenly. The charred crusty surface of the meat made it tasty. The other morsels of meat already served to the early arrivals as appetizers on paper plates had been eaten with the fingers with gusto. Sergio now turned over the cooking chore to the plump woman. Then he took off his ragged outer jacket and ragged outer pants. In his underneath red jacket and black pants he had performed for paying audiences. But now, without the exaggerated grin with which he usually warmed up an audience, he came to stand solemnly before Becky and Giancarlo, while he was breaking up inside over the great joke it seemed to him to get married on the avenue in desperate straits. "Do you take this man to be your lawful husband?" he said. "I do," said Becky. "Do you take this woman to be your lawful wife?" he said. "I do," said Giancarlo. "Then I pronounce you man and wife. You may kiss the bride, Giancarlo."

Somehow Becky Rosen had cleaned up immaculately although Sergio thought she did smell a little of turpentine. She actually looked beautiful as Giancarlo held her loosely about the waist. A Sicilian man usually didn't show too much affection for his wife in public, but Giancarlo also wouldn't allow his wife's tears to go uncomforted even though they were tears of joy. So as he held her he kissed her cheeks again and again. It had been easy for Becky to acquire this husband as she had five previous ones too, just because she always seemed so incredibly helpless that men tripped over themselves to do things for her for the reward of her beauty in their beds. But she had also tried to burn down every apartment and house she had ever lived in as a wife, and all her previous husbands had bailed out before they found themselves inside the fire. She had made a clean breast of all of that to Giancarlo before they took the big step. Giancarlo figured that there wasn't anything in their circumstances that she could burn down so he wouldn't have to worry about his own hide, and he took the plunge just so he could watch out for her and have whatever beauty she had left beside him in his bed.

"Don't cry, Becky. Everything's going to be all right," said Giancarlo. "I'm going to take care of you. Tomorrow, I'm going to the church for a bath and clean clothes. Then I'm going to find a job selling shoes again. I was the best damn salesman for ladies' shoes on 86th Street. I can do it again, Becky. In the meantime, until I get my first paycheck, Sergio said we can live down the cellar and he'll move to the hallway." Becky stopped crying and held on to Giancarlo very tight as if he would be the first husband who would truly take care of her, but then they had to let go of each other a little to accept the paper plates Sergio served them. With his hunting knife Sergio sliced the small roast and served thin pieces to all the guests, while he rehearsed in his mind the routine he would perform after everyone had a full stomach.

FIRST COUSINS

Aunt Gabriella was taken away in a straitjacket. She was taken to the madhouse. It was what my mother called it then. It was actually Kings County Hospital. Left behind were Uncle Julian and three kids. Their eldest kid had the same name as I did—Philip—both of us named after our grandfather. To tell us apart, relatives knew him as Phil the First, and me as Phil the Second. After Phil the First came Ada, his sister, then Eddie, the youngest. Ada had the face of the angel in the big oil painting in St. Finbar's. She had big brown eyes and long wavy chestnut hair. Ada, at thirteen, before going to school in the morning, and after school in the afternoon, then became a child-mother to Phil the First and to Eddie, until Uncle Julian came home at night from work. I was twelve then and held hands with Ada in the movies, and kissed her in the park.

When it seemed one afternoon there was nothing more for us to talk about, we closed the brocade drapes in the parlor and took off all our clothes. Our webs of immature pubic hair like cobwebs in the neglected parlor were stared at by both of us. Then we embraced. Our clothes, after a few minutes, were put on again. Nothing else happened. Later, after my wild women outside army posts, after my daring women at universities, after two broken marriages, after two broken live-ins, I still remembered myself at twelve with Ada at thirteen when in her parlor nothing much happened. A simple love hadn't asked for a thing. Ada grew into a beauty, and over her one guy tried to hang himself, and another tried to stab her. The guy with the knife was caught by other guys on her street who felt protective of her and they stabbed that guy with his own knife.

Ada, at thirteen, was also a whiz in math and grammar. So I asked her father if she could tutor me in math and grammar—to establish an acceptable reason to see her at her house. Four times a week we met at her house, and most days we also met after school and sometimes on secret dates. Her grammar skills were inherited, my mother said, from her crazy mother, who wrote beautiful poetry in college. And her A's in algebra were inherited from her father, an accountant at a local bank.

Unlike most men in our neighborhood, Uncle Julian didn't do backbreaking physical work. The men in our neighborhood early in life were usually worn down by their work. And Uncle Julian early in life was also worn down, not by his work, but by the absence of his wife from his bed and their home.

It was said by the Italian men of Bensonhurst, and of Little Italy too, that they were the builders of New York's skyscrapers. They were the masons, bricklayers, sheetmetal workers, electricians, plasterers, plumbers, carpenters, and contractors. And took satisfaction from that. Uncle Julian, however, had a degree. And it didn't worry him that he did paperwork instead like some of the women. And when he then became a mother hen to his motherless kids, that didn't worry him either. And it didn't worry him when at night without his wife beside him in bed he even wept like a woman. How he wept soon became known, from Ada to me, from me to my father. When Uncle Julian went to Kings County Hospital to visit his wife in a mental ward, he also smuggled in their kids to be held in the crazy woman's arms. The kids brought home-cooked dishes, new dresses Ada shopped for, and novels Uncle Julian knew she'd like. A year later Aunt Gabriella seemed much improved. So he convinced her doctor to let her out. It would soon be summer and their kids needed to be with their mother when they were home from school.

Aunt Gabriella and my own mother had gone to St. Joseph's College in Brooklyn at a time most of the other girls there were Irish. My aunt and mother were from the same neighborhood, were Italian, and soon became best friends. It was then my mother told her brother Julian how beautiful and bright Gabriella was, and introduced them. It was love at first sight. But he had to promise, before he could marry her, that their kids would go to parochial schools. My mother said that her brother to marry Gabriella then would have promised even murder.

Most Bensonhurst Italians, despite the urging of priests, didn't send their kids to parochial schools like the Irish did. Italians worried that their boys might lose their balls. And their girls might enter a convent and lose their lives. So most Italian kids were sent instead to public schools. For the neighborhood women,

Mass on Sunday mornings was often religion enough. And for the men, even Mass on Sunday mornings was too much, and was generally avoided altogether. But that summer my mother went to St. Finbar's Church a few times a week to pray for Gabriella to be restored in all her splendor to Julian and their children. If she had to be taken back to the madhouse, if she couldn't stay there at home where she was loved and wanted, then a horrible tragedy, my mother worried, awaited the entire family.

My own family lived a few blocks away. But I was more often to be found at their house. And I was there the afternoon in June when she came home from the hospital.

"I think, Phil the Second, you're possibly in love with my Ada," Aunt Gabriella said, matter-of-factly, to me the first day she was home. For a year she hadn't seen us together. For the last twenty minutes she had watched us in their backyard pouring over a magazine. Then we came inside for lemonade. "It's all right," my aunt said to us, and fondly patted our faces, while mine, I was sure, turned Irish white. "Up to a point it's all right. But you are first cousins, so it shouldn't ever become serious. I'm sure you understand."

I didn't at the time understand. The truth about my feelings for Ada—feelings I'd deny to any adult—spoken openly by her mother took my speech away. So I just nodded as if I did understand. But Ada was angry with her mother. Perhaps Ada, too, had feelings she'd deny to any adult. "Mother, he isn't in love with me," she blurted out. "I help him with grammar, and he helps me with history. How would you know anyway? You've been in the crazy house."

Aunt Gabriella wept like the mother she was. And Ada, so

self-contained during the year she'd behaved like a mother, also wept like the girl she was. They held each other and wept for a loss I had only a vague idea about. So I got out of there. And that afternoon our innocent kisses came to an abrupt end. But for years in my imagination I still kissed her.

That summer Aunt Gabriella at home was doing just fine. She was no crazier than other mothers with mischievous young children underfoot all day. Then Uncle Julian lost his job due to hard times in general, and when he wasn't looking for work, he stayed home to enjoy the presence of his wife in their home, and they were a happy family. A nighttime job as a bartender at the 19th Hole Bar then became available, the only job he could find quickly in the neighborhood to be close to home if needed. So he took the job, with his wife at home to mind their sleeping kids at night. In college his good tenor voice, and long fingers at the keyboard, earned him applause and party invitations. But he threw over his show-business ambitions as unsuitable for a family man, which he wanted to be. Those talents again came in handy as he now played the piano and sang for half-soused bar patrons who often overappreciated his performance. He was really now pretty awful. But he again earned enough to buy groceries and pay the mortgage.

One night while Uncle Julian was at work, Aunt Gabriella tried to burn the house down. Smoke reached Ada's alert little nose, and she ran out of her room and drove her brothers out of their room and phoned the fire department. But she couldn't convince her mother to leave the parlor, where the drapes and velvet sofa smoldered without flaring up. Sirens shook up the neighborhood. Neighbors poured out of their houses to witness, first, the arrival of two red fire trucks and the fire captain's sedan, then two burly firemen carrying Aunt Gabriella out of the house between them in a saddle under her made by their joined hands.

In the years that followed, Aunt Gabriella often came home from the hospital on Uncle Julian's arm for a weekend, a birthday party, or a holiday. In still later years, her children also brought her to their own homes, where she got to know her grandchildren. Her visits were usually short visits. Long visits always confirmed that she had to live out her life in a mental ward.

When Phil the First, Ada, and Eddie were still young, my mother would offer a hand in their household. And Julian would accept a hand if it wasn't too much of a hand. If it was too much, as when Mom wanted to wash all their windows, her brother would say, "Gabriella wouldn't like another woman cleaning her house. Any day now, she'll be coming home."

My mother thought that her brother's broken heart was at least partly her fault because she had made the match. That mistake could be corrected, she thought, as she tried to engineer other matches between Uncle Julian and other good and attractive women. The other women, he agreed, were indeed good and attractive. But he didn't want them. He wanted Gabriella. Those women hoped to have in their own lives a man so devoted as he was to one woman alone. Of course, if he chose one of them, that same woman wouldn't any longer consider him so desirable as a one-woman man. Uncle Julian, my father said, was a little crazy himself, because he was so devoted to his wife, even though she was locked away and couldn't give him any pleasure.

After an interval of about two years, after we found others in high school to kiss, Ada and I became friends again. And again I went to her house, to talk with Phil the First about Dodger games, but really to see Ada, to have a word or two with her. Not for long would she linger with me, and yet, during our brief exchanges, when I ached before her beauty, the core of me broken into little pieces, we both were carried away by memories of earlier days. And I went away filled up for days, until I was sweaty to see her again, and had to go back again. It was impossible to let go of her. And sometimes when I first arrived or when I was about to leave, Ada took my hand and we held hands. It wasn't much, yet it was as exciting as the adult love I made in my senior year with another girl in her basement while her mother did the weekly food shopping.

After Brooklyn College, Kathy Kelly was the girl I married. A High Mass and a big wedding were attended by hundreds of our relatives and friends, and even Aunt Gabriella came out of the hospital on Uncle Julian's arm. While she danced at the reception with her son Phil the First, I said to Uncle Julian, "She's more beautiful than ever. Is she getting any better?"

"Much, much better. She asked me to have the house painted, inside and outside, so everything will be fresh, so we'll begin fresh again." He paused to watch his wife on the dance floor. "Monday morning I'm going to see her doctor. And Monday morning the painters are coming."

"How long," I said, "has she been in there?"

"Nine years," he said.

"And," I said, "you still love her?"

"Still do," he said. "She's my wife."

I then looked over at Kathy as she waved to me from the dance floor where my father waltzed her around. Her Irish nose was so deliciously pert, her usually white cheeks were so radiant. Then I caught sight of Ada in a clutch of women relatives, and went to her and said, "How about a dance with the bridegroom, cousin?"

"I believed," she said, coming into my arms, "you'd never marry anyone but me."

"You're kidding," I said.

"Of course I am," she said. "Kathy's lovely."

Kathy was a year behind me at Brooklyn College and so graduated a year after we were married when we were already at each other's throat. It turned out we were both more in love with our studies than with each other. At a movie, in our joined hands there wasn't enough heat to suggest we had much passion for each other either. Regardless of my wish to have a child, Kathy, instead, enrolled in graduate studies at NYU, where I was too. She declared that she really didn't want to be a mother, that she, too, wanted to be a historian. Soon after, it was over for good.

Two years later I married Helen Kirschman. At the beginning it was understood that we both wanted a passel of kids. It wasn't understood by me, however, that she wanted them to be raised as Jews, that kids born of a Jewish mother and a Gentile father were considered by Jews to be Jews (while kids born of a Gentile mother and a Jewish father weren't Jews). The news that my child would be a Jew was presented to me together with the news of her pregnancy when Helen greeted me one evening with a candlelight supper. At that time I flat out didn't believe in the existence of God, and worse yet, the history of oppression all religions were guilty of made me decide that my kid wouldn't be a Jew, a Catholic, or a Muslim. He or she could choose later what, if anything, to be. So we, too, were at each other's throat for what we wanted differently. Not surprisingly, I suppose, as we sometimes slapped and kicked each other, and drank too much, and threw things, Helen miscarried. And I much later believed the universe and life were pointless without a God, so God had to exist, but God wasn't a Jew, a Catholic, or a Muslim, and didn't go to church either.

Stella, my present wife, was a former university student of mine. We have a boy eight, and a girl five, and they find their mother waiting for them at home in the afternoon after school. Mornings Stella is an editor at our university press. And evenings she helps me with grammar for my third book, about the 1861 Unification of Italy. We both now have what we want: some work for her, children for us, and teaching for me. We have, I think, a marriage which might last.

Two years ago in May my father died unexpectedly. "So he wouldn't," my mother said, "have to go with me to Denmark." We were at the funeral parlor, and instead of mourning, Mom was furious that Pop had died. "Even after he bought the tickets," she said, "I knew that somehow, at the last minute, he'd get out of it."

Pop had once loved to travel with Mom. They had visited much of Western Europe. This trip was to be to the Scandinavian countries, where they hadn't yet been, where Mom, oblivious of Pop's protest that he no longer wanted to travel, insisted was where they had to travel. In his later years, Pop had grown weary of travel, and he was done with it. He was done with Mom too, but not in any formal way, just done with her without a fuss, while he still went to bed with her every night. In his last years he wasn't really withdrawn if ignored were those contemplative silences, his thoughts pulling at a knotty problem, before he would come out of himself to laugh out loud when a contemporary of his died unexpectedly. "You know what he wanted to do all his life," Pop would say, "and never even tried to do? He wanted to go skiing once." Or "He wanted to have a beautiful young woman once." Or "He wanted to build a barbecue in his back yard." Pop remembered the unfulfilled aspirations of others and thought it was a big joke that life played on all of us, that the small things that make a life always remained unfinished.

At the funeral parlor Uncle Julian said, "Your Aunt Gabriella, she's come home now, at last."

"That's wonderful," I said.

"Her health isn't so good, but those doctors, they don't know anything," he said. "I told them, I'll take care of her myself, and she'll get better."

"I'm sure she will," I said.

"This morning, when I brushed her hair," Uncle Julian said, "you should've seen how it shined up."

"Say hello to her for me," I said.

"I will," he said. "She makes these long lists for me." He took out and studied a sheet of yellow paper. "I can certainly buy some of these things."

Ada came by and offered her condolences to my mother, then to me. I noticed that her gold wedding band wasn't on her left hand now, as she took my hand. She spoke to me softly. But her presence confused me, so I couldn't focus on what she was saying. Then she drew me to her, so I got up and went with her, the heat in her hand passing into my hand. She led me out of the room and down a hallway, unsure herself where we were going, but certain that she wanted a private place. The first two doors she tried were locked. The third opened into the display room of empty caskets with their lids propped open and their silk interiors covered by transparent plastic to keep the dust off. Ada closed the door. Her arms went around me. My arms then went around her too. We kissed long and deep, our bodies straining to connect. But we were fully dressed and the fabric between us was like the moral stricture which would always be between us.

YOUR COUNTRY WANTS YOU

"Your country, Mr. Scarlatti, is here to ask you a favor, something important," he says to me. He has a face like ten pounds of veal cutlets. He's on the porch by the door with his boys. "It's something we ourselves can't do, Mr. Scarlatti. We're in the government. It's something only a man like you can do. We'd like to come in for a minute and talk," he says.

I don't move out of his way. So he has to stay out there. He ain't no young guy. He's got a few years on him and a few pounds, like me. He has on the dark suit. In the closet I have the dark suit for when somebody gets married, somebody dies, or when I go to meet the other heads. The old heads wear the dark suit. The young ones, they wear the silk suit from the old country, but the young ones, they don't look serious. Today I work in the garden, so I have on my sweater that Millie, she knits for me, even with her arthritis.

"Hey, if you ain't got no warrant, don't bust my chops," I say. Behind him, three other guys, young guys, they keep quiet. They have almost the same face, almost the same suit. I got my own guys, two of them, in back of me, and like me, for the work out in the garden, they have on the sweater too. Millie, she knits the sweater for them. I have to keep a couple of guys around, until one of these days I go sign up for the Social Security. Millie says I should. I tell her I ain't ready. If I wait three more years to sixty-five, then I get a few more bucks. It always makes me happy to get a few more bucks. Then I say to this guy out on the porch, "My lawyer says, if you ain't got a warrant, fuck off."

"You don't understand, Mr. Scarlatti. I'm in the government, the federal government, in Washington—Dwight Gore—haven't you heard of me?"

"So what if I heard of you?" I say. I don't trust it's him. Why the hell would he be at my door? He gives me a smile but it's counterfeit, so even if it's him, he's going to give me some bullshit. You can smell bullshit before it comes out of the mouth when you get a smile that's counterfeit. Then this guy, he turns to one of his guys.

"George," he says to this young guy, "please tell Mr. Scarlatti who we are."

George comes up real close to my ear. Petey sticks his piece in George's face.

"If he makes a funny move, Petey," I say, "shoot him between the eyes." In my ear George says who this guy is, which I know, and he shows me some ID and I have to believe him. This Gore guy is a very big shit and he's here in Bensonhurst outside my house and wants to come in. I have to show my good manners. Millie says I have bad manners. She says now I get old I should have for her sake good manners. So I smile at the big shit. It's counterfeit too. He looks on my right side at my two gold teeth. The big shit himself he don't have good manners. So now I say, "Petey, Joey, take these guys to the kitchen. You have some coffee. You close the door. You keep it down, no noise." Like I make a mistake, not to have him next to me, Petey shakes his head. Petey's a little guy that long ago somebody made a mistake and cut out half his tongue. It wasn't Petey who was the rat. So I give Petey a job, and then Petey, he cut out not only the tongue but the eyes too that did it to him. Petey ain't so nice. For me he's like a Doberman dog. "It's okay, Petey. But first you frisk them."

"We're not the police, try to understand that," says George. "We don't carrry guns. Okay, for heaven's sake, go ahead, frisk us."

In the parlor the big guy sits in my chair. Right away I can see he's an asshole. He don't take into account it's my house. So I shake my finger. Then I point to the sofa. So he goes to the sofa. The big chair is my chair. When I tell somebody what to do I sit in my chair. The other guy, when he has to do what I say, he has to sit down on the sofa. Before I sit down I go pour some scotch. One inch for him and for me. Then I sit in my chair with my drink. And he sits on the sofa with his drink.

"My doctor says, for the veins I could have in the morning one shot, in the night one shot," I tell this guy. "If I have more it ain't good. If you ask me, nothing's too good to drink or eat anymore." He don't look too comfortable. It ain't the sofa. It's something in him. He's got under his eyes bags like in the old country they used to put the wine in a bladder from a goat. He's got two bladders under his eyes.

"Me too, I have a few medical problems," he says. "At our

age, I guess almost everyone does." He get up and walks here and walks there. "Is it okay to talk about important matters, without being overheard?"

"It's okay, I swear. Maybe my Millie, she comes in. But my Millie, she don't hear nothing."

"Is your wife hard of hearing?" he says when he sits down again.

"Not my Millie. In the house next door, my granddaughter, if she cries at two in the morning, my Millie, she could hear that. She hears things like that. About what I do, you know, my work, she don't hear nothing. Years ago we worked it out. So, you came here all the way from Washington by car? That ain't no short drive up the block."

"Actually, Tommaso—is it okay if I call you Tommaso?—we came by plane. And please call me D.G."

He gets very friendly now and calls me by my first name. I don't like that. First you must be a true friend before you can use a man's first name. Dwight Gore is not my true friend. But for now I have to play his game, so I say, "Sure, you call me Tommaso, I call you D.G."

"Well, Tommaso, here in New York, we have people, offices, and cars too. But this business will be just between you and me, and George. George knows about it, but no one else. It's an operation you know how to carry out very efficiently. For example, we know that in World War II, in Salerno, you were a hero. I have a list of your medals."

"Those sonofabitch Nazis they screwed up my old country. Mussolini too, fascist bastard. So I have to kill one or two, no? But I don't like to kill nobody."

"At times, we have to, if someone's trying to hurt us. Or

hurt our country," D.G. says, and right away I smell dirty business. "Only a man like you can do this for our country. We know you're a patriotic man, Tommaso. For example, on legal holidays, you show the flag on your house. And your son, when pickets were in front of the courthouse—well, the government appreciates his loyalty too."

D.G. gets up from the sofa again, and goes to the window. Then he comes back and stands by my chair. "Maybe you've heard, Tommaso—the Brooklyn D.A., that Italian woman, will be sending up some heavy indictments on you. She intends to nail you this time. I can do you a big favor?"

"That's very nice," I say.

"To put it bluntly, we want a certain man taken out," says D.G.

"I ain't in that business," I say. "I'm in the insurance business. Maybe you mix me up with somebody else. Us Sicilian guys, people, they think we're all in the old business, but we ain't."

Right then Millie, she comes in. She brings these little glasses of Marsala, and a bowl of peanuts without the salt. She don't let me have the salt. So I say, "Millie, meet this here guy, he comes from Washington." She shakes his hand and he says something to her and she answers in Sicilian, because she never talks in American to nobody except her granddaughter. It's like not only she don't hear in American, but also she can't even say nothing in American, which is bullshit, because everything she understands. For the wine and the nuts, I say to Millie, "Grazie," and she goes out. But I think she leaves in the room her ears. That's not so bad, because maybe, after, I have some questions to ask Millie about this guy who comes from Washington.

"Well, Tommaso, if you're not the right man for this covert action, then, let's just say, for the sake of your country, for this one time, will you consider becoming the right man?" he says. "There's a colonel, in charge in his own country, who's a headache. The only way to get rid of him is with guerrilla diplomacy. These troublemakers threaten peace in the world, stability and democracy in their own countries." He finishes his drink. "I can't send my own men; it's against the law. But you and I know that for a good cause, it's important sometimes to bend the law. For example, we know that you have a large income from gambling, whorehouses in Harlem, protection, extortion, even hijacking. But you also contribute to Catholic Charities very large sums of cash to help the homeless."

"Who, me?"

"Everything you'll need, Tommaso—passports, papers, money, connections, weapons, safe houses, and transportation—everything will be worked out for your convenience and safety. But—and this is very important—we want you to be there yourself, for a professional job; no blunders. Take three or four of your people. Joey, we know, is your marksman. You were a marksman yourself, Tommaso, back in Salerno. How many was it, forty-seven?"

"It was only one or two," I say. "And I never kill nobody else. You got the wrong guy, D.G."

Then he gets up and he comes to shake my hand. "George will come around to see you in a few weeks. He'll bring the passports and tell you a little more. Whatever you need, George will take care of it. I won't see you again, Tommaso, so I wish you good luck. I want you to know that this could be the most heroic thing, even more than Salerno, that you'll do for your country. Your country wants you," he says to me, like he's Uncle Sam in the poster in World War II who wants a guy to join up.

"I'm sorry, D.G., but you got yourself the wrong guy. I ain't done no hit before. I just sell insurance to a young couple so, God forbid, he dies, she has enough money to raise their kid." The sonofabitch, he thinks he has me over the barrel. I hear about the indictments, but I don't lose no sleep. A witness, or a guy on the jury, he could always get a few bucks and change his mind, or he could, God forbid, walk into a car goes too fast.

"Personally, I would give you a medal, Tommaso, for just being a loyal American. But the D.A. wants to put you in jail. We think she's slightly on the pink side."

"She ain't too bad-looking. Smart too," I say. "But like you, she's got the wrong guy. Look at me here, I'm a guy who digs in the garden to plant the green peppers, the eggplants."

In the old days it would take me two minutes to make up my mind if it's the colonel or if it's D.G. who should get hit. Now it takes me longer to make up my mind. After he goes out the door with his guys, I go out back to the garden with my guys. My guys, they don't ask me nothing, and I don't tell them nothing. It's better not to worry your guys with a problem. It's better just to give them how you solved it. Some guys can't stand a problem on their minds. Me, for years, I like a problem, I like to figure it out, so I come out on top. It stinks on the bottom. In the old days I make a lot of mistakes when I decide too fast what to do. Now I don't take the first idea I get. My guys, they whisper that I'm the gray fox. But I'm not so smart as they think. To come up with an answer, sometimes, I have to get down on my knees to ask God what to do. God, He don't talk to me no more. But I talk to Him. I tell Him it's only the scum that I hit. He wouldn't let those bastards in heaven anyway.

That night Petey and Joey, they don't stay for dinner with me and Millie when she asks them to sit down with us. It's Saturday night and they say they go to a wedding reception. But the guys who come on for the night, they're late. So, at the last minute, Petey, he stays, and Joey, he goes. It turns out two hours later the other guys get stopped for going fast, which is a joke, since I tell my guys not to go fast, the cops, they just wait to stop you, they know you work for me. Then my guys show up and then Petey too goes to the wedding. For dinner Millie makes in the sauce with the pasta, the baccalà, the dried-up cod from Sicily. First we have the escarole with the oil and the garlic. To keep down for me the cholesterol, she cooks what the doctor says. I hate the doctor. I hate the liar. I hate the cheat. I hate the lawyer. I hate the guy from the government. I don't feel so good either about the funeral director.

"I didn't hear you say today that Frankie called," I say. Millie is very quiet. She is not always so quiet. Millie is like my eyes and my ears. What she hears on the radio that I should know, on TV, in the magazine, she tells me. What goes on in the neighborhood, what goes on in politics, around the world even, she tells me. I think she should run for president. "I didn't hear either that your daughter Frances, she called."

"Nobody called," says Millie. "I don't want to say nothing bad about that girl who Frankie married, that Dolores. But I think, when Frankie was asleep, that Dolores cut off a piece of his salami, and now he's Jewish too. He forgets all about his family." Millie is crazy about the son we have, but he has his own life now, which she don't understand. Frankie plays the trombone and Dolores always goes where he plays, to Chicago, to San Francisco. I like that Dolores.

"Is that why you so quiet tonight, because nobody called?" I say.

"I'm not quiet tonight," she says.

"I don't hear you talking."

"I have on my mind some things," she says.

"What's on your mind, Millie?"

"Some things, Tommaso."

"I think you worry about your daughter Frances. If I could find the guy who gives her that bambino, I would fix him up good," I tell her.

"I don't want you to fix him up," she says.

"You worry because she don't have no husband, she has just the baby. What can you do with kids today?"

"I don't worry about Frances," she says. "Frances tells me she don't want to marry the boy. She says the boy is smart, he looks handsome, but he's a crook like her father, like you, Tommaso. It's what she says. She's mad at you."

"It's the only thing I know how to do, Millie. Pretty soon I hang up my hat. Then we go down to Florida. We get a little place. We get a little boat. We play a little bocce with the old folks."

"Frances will be okay," Millie says. "Frances graduated from the university. She knows everything."

"So, it's not Frankie, it's not Frances, so what's on your mind, Millie?"

"Nothing's on my mind, Tommaso."

About two weeks later when George calls up, Millie tells him in Sicilian in the same way she tells anybody who calls up for me that I'm not home. Anybody calls up I'm never home. I ask Millie if she wants me to get one of those machines it could answer the phone instead of her. She says it's better she answers it herself because she can hear in the voice of the person something about what he wants, but on a machine everybody talks with the same voice. She knows that because Frances next door has a machine. One day goes by, two days, I can't make up my mind if I should take care of the colonel, if it's so important for my country. It's hard to know sometimes what's important and what's bullshit. There's a very fine line. Another problem I have is I hate to do business with a sonofabitch personally I don't give a shit for—Dwight Gore. In me he pushes the wrong button. I don't know why. He don't spit on my floor. Just I don't trust the guy. To me trust is more important than love. I don't trust nobody except for Millie. Millie I put my life in her hands.

Then I make up my mind to call back George. So I call him. I say my name is Sam Smith. George said when I call back I should say I'm Sam Smith. Do I sound like Sam Smith? Asshole. "Hey, George, how the hell are you? It's Sam Smith. Yeah, I'm fine. Let me see, let me think about this—when would be a good time—how about next week? Thursday night. I know it's dark Thursday *night.* It's better it's dark. I'll leave on the porch light. Your guys coming too? Good. My Petey gets nervous when he sees too many guys come up to the door."

From the supermarket Millie comes back with Petey and Joey loaded up. Jesus, she buys enough to feed a whole mob. It's no wonder I have on me a few pounds. I'm not fat. A little plump around the middle. Us Sicilians, we eat too much. I don't know why. Maybe it has to do with the old country where we just had some olives, some oranges, a crust of bread.

Petey stocks up the refrigerator, and Joey the pantry. They help out Millie. They don't mind I send them with her to the store. And she don't mind. It's like they in the family. I don't worry too much that some young punk puts me out of business. First, I don't go to the restaurants where mostly they make the hit. Sometimes a guy gets hit when he shacks up with a broad, she ain't his wife. I never in my life cheat with a broad. But I myself had to hit one guy when back forty years ago I had to make my bones, the guy, he screwed the wife of a boss. The worst part was, after I hit him, I had to cut off his cock and stick it in his mouth. I didn't like that part. It was a message to the other guys. The woman, she didn't have hurt one hair on her head. But the boss, he told her she had to go in the convent. If she ever came out, she was dead. So she went in. She's still in there. She must be about eighty. Nobody's going to hit her anymore.

"Hey, you guys, go out in the yard, have a beer, cool off a minute. I want to have a word with my wife here," I tell them. They always listen to me. I like them guys. I don't think they would run out on me if an army pulled up. A guy like me, when the shit comes down, he can't always be sure. Some sonofabitches I heard about, they run like scared rabbits. "I don't know, Petey, if the door is locked. Please, you go see for yourself."

Because Petey can't talk he has this way where he points and he makes a funny noise and I feel like I been trained by him to understand him. Petey carries more iron on him than I ever heard any guy carries. He carries an Uzi. He carries a .357 magnum. He carries a little derringer on his ankle. He carries knuckles in his pocket. He carries a blackjack in his back pocket.

In his belt he has a knife in front, a knife in back. He can't wait to get his hands on somebody. He'll make sausage out of somebody. Sometimes I think I have to throw him somebody like a bone just so he don't want to get me by mistake. It's been a long time since I've thrown him somebody. One of these days I have to set Petey up with a legit business, a bar maybe, when I quit myself, or maybe I have to adopt him if he don't want a legit business.

What I ask Petey to do is stay in the closet when George comes over. If George acts funny, if it's all a setup, Petey can shoot him. What I ask Millie to do is to bring in some coffee and macaroons. She nods. I think she wants to say something about George. But she don't say boo. So I say, "Do you have an opinion, Millie?" She looks at me in the same way as when she hears some merchandise, it comes on the boat from Palermo, which, with her ears, she don't hear.

"The only reason that I suggested that we might meet on the pedestrian path near Gravesend Bay," George says, "was because I thought it would be the most private place." After he sits down on the sofa he opens his briefcase, and I keep an eye on his hand when it comes out of the briefcase. Only papers come out. "Law enforcement, as we suggested the last time, Mr. Scarlatti, is very interested in you. There was always a possibility that your house was bugged, besides your telephone, which definitely was bugged. One of our people took care of that. To be sure it was clean in here, we set up a microwave around your house. We didn't find any bugs in your house. The bug on the phone was on an outside wire."

"I have a genius who works for me, he takes care of any bugs," I tell him. "Once a week he comes in and sweeps up the place.

For two years he ain't found nothing. So, whatever you have to say, nobody hears it but me."

"What about your wife, and your bodyguards?"

"My wife, and my guys, and me, we make the holy trinity, three in one. We're all the same person—me. Are you a religious man, George?" He gives me a little smile, and I see he's a little nervous; maybe, for coming here, he could go to jail. "Let's see what you got, George."

"We took the liberty of making some passports, for you, for Petey and Joey, and for your driver. And we gave you some new names, Spanish names."

I look at the pictures, at the passports. I can't believe how they get them. "You snoop around here to take these here pictures? What else you guys been up to? You guys I think are pretty dangerous," I say to George. He likes to hear that. "What country is this guy in we're supposed to rub out?"

"I can't tell you that, Mr. Scarlatti. It's not important for you to know that," George says. "The man is a threat to our country; and a threat to freedom in his own country. He's a murderer too."

"That don't seem like enough reason to kill a guy," I tell him. "Maybe he has some good qualities. Maybe he helps out the orphans. Loves his wife and mother. Goes to church."

"I think you're joshing with me, Mr. Scarlatti. This is important business. I thought your mind was made up."

"Okay, George, I got my mind made up. I do the job," I tell him. "How do I get to this country?"

"A small airline that we control will take you there. It flies out of Florida," says George. "When you arrive in that country, locals in our employ will take you to a safe house. You'll be briefed there. It's a national holiday or something. The colonel will make a speech. That's when you'll take him out."

"If you got on the scene your local guys, then how come you need me?" I ask him.

"They just collect information, Mr. Sacrlatti. They don't know how to do what you know how to do. We need a pro. And secrecy. They don't know what's going to happen. The locals are amateurs, even when they try to get information," George says. "From our research on your background, Mr. Scarlatti, we learned that you don't leave loose ends. In your business, you rarely make a mistake. Mr. Gore, who, I guess you've heard, isn't too well, admires you immensely. Mr. Gore said that you could've been a leader of industry if you had been in industry."

When somebody gives me the pat on the back I worry that in the other hand he has the gun, or the wire for the piano. "Yeah, I hear about Mr. Gore on TV. What's the matter with him? Is the guy sick, or is it some operation he's up to?"

"He went to the hospital for some tests. I talked to him this morning. He's feeling fine, and asked me to remind you that what you're doing for your country becomes more important every day. We can't ever talk about it, of course."

Millie serves the coffee and the cookies and turns down her eyes like she is the maid instead of the lady of the house. But she don't fool me. She hears every word. Then she goes out. For one minute, me and George, we have the coffee, and I think about Petey in the closet so long. Poor Petey, he maybe has to take a leak by now. But still he has to wait, the way Joey, he waits by the front door to be sure nobody else comes in.

"What about the cops in that country, the army?" I say to George, like I'll do this thing. "How about when it's time to leave there, to come home? You got a plan to get us out?"

"Certain officials have been bribed," says George.

"I got to have the guarantee that my guys don't get hurt. That I don't get hurt, George. I need the guarantee."

"I'm not sure I understand, Mr. Scarlatti. We'll do everything humanly possible to see you get back here safely. You have my word on that."

"Fuck your word. Let me tell you something, George—if we don't come back in one piece, I got some friends, they come to find *you*. You, George. Then you have to pay the bill, with your life. So you make sure that me and my guys, we come back."

"I'll make sure, Mr. Scarlatti."

After George goes away I feel myself stuck in my chair; that I can't get up on my feet, because I have a heavy problem for which I don't have the answer. If I don't do the job, the D.A. will be on my back. That would make Millie very sad. And it won't be good for my guys either, unless I beat the rap. It's possible. I got a good mouthpiece, another dame like the D.A. It takes one cat to scratch out the eyes of another cat. No dog could do it. So I have this dame and she's a looker, and she's got the smarts, and she grew up in this same neighborhood, Bensonhurst. She has two kids too.

If I get mixed up with these government guys, if I do the job, these guys will be on my back for the rest of my life. They will come back for another favor. They will have me by the balls. It makes me crazy. If this was just a hit over business, I could talk it over with my goombas; some of them got more experience. This is different. I don't know what to call this. There's nobody to talk to about this, unless I talk to Millie.

When I go in the kitchen Millie bakes the bread for Easter.

She makes the dough in twists with the color eggs hardboiled inside so it looks like a basket of eggs. She does this for almost forty years. I can't even eat no more the eggs. For a couple of days she likes to look at it. Then she gives it away to other people so they can eat it for Easter, which comes next week. If I don't keep my eye on Millie she gives away the whole house. I tell her she should of been a nun. She tells me she couldn't be no nun because she still has for me the hots. She makes me laugh.

"Please, Tommaso, can you take out the trash?" she says. "The trash is piled up here, it looks like a mountain. Before I asked Petey. But Petey don't like to take it out."

"It's my job, Millie," I say. "I don't want you to give my job to Petey. How would I know I was the man of the house if Petey takes it out?" It's sort of a joke between Millie and me. When I go outside by the trash cans I see across the street a car with two guys in the front seat. It's the same car D.G. and his guys, they came in. The two guys, they have on these suits. So I wave. Then they wave. I guess they want to keep me nice and pure. I figure in the house and on the phone I got bugs now that maybe my own genius, he can't find. It's lucky I take out the trash. You never know when you take out the trash how it can turn into a lucky break. In the kitchen again I turn up the radio that Millie keeps nice and low but I like to hear nice and loud when it's the opera. "I want you to leave everything here and let's go out to the garden. I can't figure out what to do about this problem." Then I tell her everything, but I see in her eyes she knows everything.

"The country can be in Central America, or in South America, or even in Africa, the Middle East, Southeast Asia. It can be anywhere, Tommaso," she says. "From what I read in the newspaper, the world is full of colonels who are bad people. Maybe he isn't really a colonel. In some countries it can be a general. In other countries it can even be a president. You shouldn't do it, Tommaso. It's better that you go to the court and face the D.A. I'll be there with you."

"For myself, Millie, I don't mind if I go to jail. But I don't want to go away from you. You need me here." My wife, she takes my hand like we are two young chickens. "But I won't go to no jail, Millie. I never been in one in all my life."

"I think you shouldn't trust this George, and that Dwight Gore. I think, these men, they're criminals. That what they do is a crime, Tommaso."

"Maybe sometimes the government, to do something good, has to do first something bad," I say to her. "For democracy, we have to do it."

"What I think, Tommaso, is, you should go to the hospital too, like Dwight Gore," says Millie. "I'll call up the doctor. The doctor knows what to do. He'll send the ambulance, like the last time, and you'll have a vacation."

We go back to the kitchen, where Millie makes for me a big dish of macaroni which my doctor, he says it's okay to have, and Millie puts in the mushrooms, the olives, the green peas, and the anchovies. Then we sit down to eat, but no more we talk about the dirty business.

On Good Friday Millie goes to St. Finbar's for the Passion from twelve o'clock to three o'clock, when Christ dies on the cross. That's when I get a visit again from George, with the guns. He brings me a present too. He says he knows I love a good cigar. He's got the connection to get the havanas from

Cuba even though our country and Cuba, we have no trade. He says that he himself went to Cuba in a small boat and stayed there one year undercover. "I'll do anything for my country, Mr. Scarlatti," he says. "And we're very pleased that you too will serve your country as you did in the war. You will help to bring peace in one small corner of the world. Then we can have military bases there. It's very important."

Myself I hate to go to church. I'm sorry that Christ, He dies on the cross, but there's nothing I can do. So I stay home, and Millie, before she goes to church, she makes me the nice lunch. She makes the octopus. So I say to George, "You like the octopus? Come in the kitchen, George, you try the octopus. We have some Sicilian bread with the hard crust. We have some wine. And we have the artichokes. To take off one leaf at a time it's a pain in the ass, but it's worth it, it's got a nice flavor. You try it, George."

After Easter when my son Frankie and my daughter Frances, they don't come home to see us, the rotten kids, not that I care for myself, but for Millie I care, then me and Millie, we decide it's time, the next day, for me to go to the hospital. She calls up on the phone the doctor who is my friend from when we both grew up in Bensonhurst. She says to Dr. Vito Conti one word special so he understands it's the same deal that when he put me in the hospital so I don't have to talk to the attorney general of the state. It's like a code. In the hospital Dr. Vito Conti comes in when I'm in the bed and he asks me what hurts and I give him the answers. The next two days I take some tests for my heart. Then George shows up just the way I figure it. I tell Petey it's all right for George to come in, but Petey, he should keep out any other guys. I tell Petey not to worry about

George. Under the sheet I have a gun that's quiet.

"Mr. Scarlatti, how're you feeling?"

"I feel lousy, George. I think I'm going to die," I tell him, and without a shave for two days, and without the hairs pulled out by Millie from my nose, my ears, my eyebrows, I look a little bit like a dead body. To get old is to die every day a little bit. I hate to get old. I hate to die. "I'm sorry, George, I don't know what to say."

"Actually, Mr. Scarlatti, there's been a change in plans," he says. "It's not going to be necessary to take out the colonel. But I still want to take advantage of our friendship. I want another favor, in exchange for suppressing the indictments."

"What about the colonel?" I say. A week ago the colonel is so important, now he's not so important. I can't believe it. These assholes, they don't think too clear with their heads; either a guy has to go or not, there's no in-between when it comes to a hit.

"Well, it was Dwight Gore's idea to take out the colonel. It's my idea to apply instead certain economic pressures. I'm acting chief now," says George. "And I have a more serious problem than the colonel. I have to worry now about D.G. himself. He's become an old fool."

I don't have to ask what the problem is. It's the same in my business. The acting chief, he don't want to be just the acting chief. He has to speed things up. He has to get rid of the big chief. I did it myself. I knocked off the chief of my family so I could be the chief. But now I'm sixty-two, and it's time to retire, so I have to keep Petey and Joey around to make sure that my own acting chief, he don't put a hit on me. I think when I get out of the hospital I tell Millie that once and for all

I get out of the business. I turn it over to Alfredo before he has to give me the hit.

"I'm throwing in a bonus, Mr. Scarlatti, a hundred thousand dollars."

"Whatever the problem is with D.G.," I say, "I can't do nothing to help you out, George. I'm a very sick man."

"D.G. is babbling. I worry about his babbling," says George. "He's dying, and saying all kinds of things, spilling his guts."

"You're talking big stuff here, George. You're talking about a guy who you told me yourself in my ear is very important in this country. You can't do nothing to a guy who is very important like that."

"He's even mentioned your name, Mr. Scarlatti. Twice. That's not good for you. Or for the country. Or to have these secrets come out in the newspapers, on TV around the world."

"How could he be dying?" I say. "I just saw him, when was it, a little over a month ago."

"He's had this thing for years, but now it's out of control," says George. "He can only last another week or two. The way we'll do it is, I'll smuggle in your Petey, dressed like a doctor. Then I'll smuggle him out again."

"Why can't you do it yourself?" I tell him.

"I can't go in his room alone. We have to go in two at a time, it's the rule. But if Petey pretends to be a doctor, we can go in together. It has to look like a natural death. No blood, no marks, no drugs. You understand?"

"I understand," I tell him.

"One more thing, Mr. Scarlatti. It has to be done right away. I want you to tell Petey right away while I wait out in the hall. Tell him to come with me. I'll drive him right now to Washington and the hospital. When it's finished I'll drive him back. For your cooperation, Mr. Scarlatti, I personally guarantee, for as long as I'm chief—no indictments. We can be friends for a long time."

"I like that, George, very much. Shake hands on that. You my good friend. I sent Petey to go with you. But first, he must call some other guys, to be here when he goes away. I like to have some guys in my room. You come back in one hour. Then I send Petey. You tell Petey to come in and I tell him. Take care of yourself, George. God bless you for the good work you do to keep me out of jail."

When Petey comes in I ask him to sit down for a minute. Then I ask the nurse to bring me and him some coffee without the caffeine. She puts me up on the pillow. Then I sip my coffee and I look inside my eyes. Then I know what to do. Petey has to go with him. There's no in-between for George. "Petey, drop George off in Jersey, in the swamp," I say and close my eyes.

IN DELPHINE'S BED

"It ain't no pipe dream. Hey, you ever remember even once you didn't hear the truth from me? It was always the truth I told you. And it's the truth now—I'm going to make a killing, and I'll share it with you, all of it. Half a million ain't mashed potatoes," said Roselli.

Half a dozen women had seen Roselli pack his bag and take off—their cologne gagging him when it became too familiar, their hands at a show or a bar making his clammy—but that was before Delphine. One day she walked by like that pretty doll no little boy of five ever gets to play with, her mouth so rosy, and Roselli wanted to stick his tongue in her mouth without even saying hello first. And now in Rocky's Royal Flush—a joint with a nightly floor show on a side street off the boardwalk—Roselli happily held her hand, and was breathing in as much of her cologne as his lungs could hold.

"Half a million could keep us pretty good, but you have to button your rosy lips, and we have to haul ass out of town soon as the golden egg is laid," said Roselli. "I'll take real good care of you, sugar, and give you a soft pillow for your pretty head. What more could you want?"

The cravings of a woman recently twenty and almost a decade his junior were unknown to him aside from her desire never to be homeless on the boardwalk like the hundreds passing by every day. A buck in her purse stayed in there until the rent was long overdue and then she would part with it like with a best friend. What else she might want wasn't in the crystal balls of her eyes; her eyes didn't even have that billboard hype that a woman working in a boardwalk joint needed for promoting herself to something better. It didn't matter that her eyes were as empty as glass; their pale color and their big size put Roselli in a trance anyway.

"It's hard to believe you when you say your mind's going to blow up and splatter on the wall because you love me so much and can't have me for good, gee," said Delphine. "You have to talk like a normal person, who knows what's the score, which you do, Roselli. I'll be glad to go away with you, but I'm a poor working girl, and you're a working bookie, and that ain't no future for nobody."

The permanent place Roselli wanted in her underpants was reserved for some other really classy guy worth a million when he came along, she said, and so far Roselli had failed on both counts. Roselli had hair on his chest and made her laugh and dressed to kill and was no cheapskate (any woman hated a tight fist, were her words), and even though she loved him, she had been around enough to know that love was more or less a passing condition, like dandruff. One morning she might wake up and find herself, without a moment's notice, in love with the saxophonist instead.

Roselli whispered to her the words of a guy light-headed over a luscious colleen who thought about herself that she was only one petal prettier than the ordinary woman, which made Roselli love her even more. Something else Roselli breathed into her perfumed ear—a hint of the rip-off that had crossed his mind and should also have been tossed out fast and unspoken, even by a dreamer. Just thinking it could burn a hole in one's brain. The idea could be suicidal for almost anyone else, he thought, but not too risky for him. The high-voltage gamble of bookmaking already gave him the chance to come up a prince someday, depending on how the ponies ran, and even though on some really bad days he came up a pauper, he never went into shock over it. If his scheme failed, he could handle that too. The odds weren't in his favor, he figured, but then, big money was never made on the sure thing but always on the longshot.

"Okay. It's a deal. I'm trusting you, Roselli," said Delphine. "But I hope it ain't no con you're giving me, because I can't stand no guy with a con, when once I find him out. So, if the dough ain't there, I'm coming right back here. Otherwise I need this job. And I ain't even asking you, because, to tell the truth, I don't want to know exactly, how you're getting it. But gee, I'm going to love you to bits if you do get it, and help you watch over it like a hawk, and we can live like human beings, and not have to work our tails off. A person's entitled to a good time in life, it's over so fast. My mother, booze killed her, and my daddy fell off a tall building, they said. I love you, Roselli, but I hope, sure as hell, that you're straight with me."

The next morning Roselli was to take in two quarter-of-a-million-dollar bets, a hundred times as much together as he took in in a normal day. What usually happened when he took in bets concentrated on one horse or larger than he could handle was he laid off some of the money to the other bookies he knew, since he hadn't yet built up enough capital to pay off bets over four figures. The horse at the center of his ploy was King Ransom. It was the favorite and no doubt about it it was going to win, since the race was fixed besides. That tip had come from a friend at the track on Roselli's fifty-dollar gift list once a month. The tipster then let the word out at Roselli's suggestion to the other bookies around town for a hundred apiece.

Those few jockeys in the race who had a distant chance of winning had been paid off by Jimmy "Mash Potatoes" Kelly, and Reno "Poison" Polito. They were buddies and the major pimps in town, but the big-money bookies wouldn't take their bets on King Ransom now, and the average-bet bookies—even forgetting they knew the race was loaded—wouldn't ever cover a big bet. The only bookie around who seemed dumb enough to take their bets was Roselli, so Jimmy and Reno had to do business with him.

Without a lying blush in his barroom pallor, Roselli promised those guys that he could cover their bets. Any bookie who wanted to go on taking bets, and not have his legs broken besides, always had to pay off when he lost. Roselli had that reputation—he never welshed on a bet. In fact, if a bettor was cleaned out of his last dollar, Roselli was known for handing over his own money to the guy, probably a fifty for dinner and a cheap room for the night, or for gas to get out of town before he lost his shirt too.

And when a bettor called on the phone or stopped by in

person to place a bet, Roselli always wished the gambler good luck, as if he was on the gambler's side instead of on the other side, his side. But the gambling business made Delphine a little nervous. Living on the edge of financial collapse all her young life, she saved a dollar whenever she could, and worried that Roselli might lose the fortune he was planning to get on bets he would make himself. "My mother told me in a dream that once I get my hands on a nest egg I should protect it with my life, if I didn't want to end up in a bad hole, like she was in when she died," Delphine said to Roselli. But he swore to her that he never placed a bet, which wasn't the whole truth. His taking bets was almost the same as the other guys making them, except if he could take bets on all the horses in a race, the five or six that lost usually guaranteed money in his pocket, even if he had to pay off the winner. One of a dozen possibilities, however, could always go wrong, and it did a couple of times a day.

Most weekdays, the bettors put down their fins, sawbucks, C-notes with Roselli, and dreamed that a winning stallion could change their lives for more than twenty-four hours, but Roselli observed that it never did. Always there were other nags to bet on.

Roselli had grown up in the Sicilian neighborhood of Bensonhurst, where it took a little extra guts not to get caught forever in the grind of going up to the elevated in the morning and coming down again at night from a job that would at least bend his back, and then, to forget his burden, he would drink too much wine, which would give him his father's paunch too. As a bookmaker, he made a pretty good living, but it was still just a job, and he could still get hunched over from a year in the slammer, and still get broken down from the lousy eating habits of a bookie on the street. Another danger could come from some bettor or from some other bookie who might try to clean him out of his last dollar with a flimflam, as he himself was planning to do, so every day he had to pay strict attention to what was going on.

It wasn't that Roselli loved money, or that he was tired of taking bets every day, or that he thought he was a genius and could stick it to some big turds and get away with it. The big score was in his dreams simply because he knew from Delphine's own lovely mouth, and found it to be true in her heart too, that she was a woman who just had to find a guy with a fat roll in his pocket. No matter how wonderful and handsome he was, she just wouldn't love him for keeps if he was Mr. Ordinary. So Roselli just had to get a roll, he was that buggy about her, that willing to risk his neck—their necks—in a scam that he hoped and prayed would go off without a hitch. Then he would get her for good, the only woman he had ever desperately wanted, and keep her the way she needed to be kept.

His tie was black from his Bensonhurst days and it made a nice contrast with his baby-blue outfit, which included even his shirt. The black tie hinted that deep inside him, beneath his layers of silk and smiles, joker and good sport, could be a very serious guy who kept a small-caliber Beretta in the drawer under his shirts, as if he was truly his father's son; that he too could plug a guy between the eyes if it came to that, but Roselli hoped that he too wouldn't get sent up for life.

Delphine believed he was tough enough to protect her from the apes who wanted a handful; the creeps who would pay big money to dip their bills in her sugar. Her man not only had to be all man, which Roselli was, not only had to have tons of money, which Roselli might have any day, but he should also have a little class, which was where Roselli fell down. But she could overlook the Brooklyn kid still in his speech, the way he stuck his chin out, throwing his fists when necessary. In fact, she liked it that he was a little dangerous, and Roselli thought he was too. At the back of his mind, however, he wasn't sure that the cold streak was in him to pull the trigger of the Beretta. Sure, he could smash some mean bastard in the mouth who came on too strong to any woman of his over the years, but that was all he had done. He never even had the heart to beat up those gamblers he gave credit to who then welshed on him, but they taught him some lessons.

Lesson Number One was to take the big-money bets only in hard currency, no credit, no notes, no jewelry, nothing but green stuff. So when Jimmy "Mash Potatoes" Kelly called him at Rocky's Royal Flush where Roselli took in his bets, Roselli was ready to tell his stories of how high rollers had welshed on him before, but how he had never welshed on them, so any bet with him had to be in good old American lettuce. If Jimmy wasn't interested he could take his bet elsewhere, which there wasn't any elsewhere to go to for that bet. It sounded good not to give a damn one way or another.

After Jimmy sent in his bet with the black giant in thick glasses, Bottle Eyes, who cut people with a straight-edged razor for Jimmy when it was deemed necessary, the only unexpected thing that happened the morning of the race was that Reno showed up at Rocky's in person, with his 250 Gs in a shopping bag.

"I want to know where you're going to be so I could come over and collect my bet when the race is over and I win," said

Reno, who smelled like a pansy and was rumored to be one, but nobody ever provided the evidence, possibly for fear that Reno might lose his temper. He spoke softly—"This here bundle that I'm trusting you with, Roselli, I'm expecting to get back in one piece, plus some more that I'm going to win, so nothing should happen to it. No great idea should come into your head."

"Hey, Reno, you ever hear I didn't pay off a winning bet? I'm solid as Chase Manhattan. Your money's in safe hands with me. Even the cops watch out I don't get robbed by no two-bit hood coming in. Good luck on your bet, Reno. And if you win, you can find me here at Rocky's at six, and I'll pay you off in dollar bills, the same way you're betting."

The usual morning jelly doughnut Roselli left untouched, and he also resisted his usual cigarette between his fingers, which was part of his outfit, which he might puff just once or twice, but which looked nice, he thought. The smoke was resisted because he didn't want to look nervous when he definitely felt like coming apart inside, but he looked calm, looked so sure of himself, so pale. His color, or rather the lack of it, in his face helped him in his work, suggested his purity perhaps, which ordinarily existed in this gambling city only in a glass of milk, but which everyone hoped could exist in the next guy, or the next doll, or in the bookie.

"I got backers," Roselli told Reno again. "Casino bigshots. They're my partners. When some guy comes up a big winner, they come up with the cash. So you don't have to give it a thought, Reno. I already let them know the size of your bet, and they said—Absolutely, Positively, There ain't no problem, You're covered."

Reno's red eyes from too much booze normally were hidden

in little slits like fresh scars caused by his meatball cheeks pushing up almost into his forehead, but now his eyes almost disappeared entirely in his squint that suggested he was measuring Roselli for his casket in case Roselli was lying through his teeth, which of course he was. Almost all the crooked ideas one could think of on the boardwalk had already been dredged up by Reno's imagination without him ever needing instruction from ex-cons. He was rotten by nature, *poison* everyone said, but it paid good, and there wasn't anything hardly, or anyone, Reno couldn't buy.

The only thing Reno wanted more of was money. The only thing he worried about was that he might lose a dollar he already had. That worry could give him a pain in his belly which urged him to eat meatballs by the dozen in one sitting, which made him fatter still. Reno Polito now patted Roselli on his dark, thick, brushed-back hair that was groomed to have a shine. He patted Roselli's head like a Sicilian father would his son's head, not so much as a warning to do the right thing, but almost to press into his brain a vital fact of life. Under no circumstances should that fact be forgotten or ignored. But Roselli was already ignoring it—that Reno would come and find him if he skipped out with his bet. The East Coast was a big place, teeming with millions of people, and every day some of them walked out the door and got lost in the crowd, thought Roselli, just as he and Delphine would get lost, and he watched the fat man waddle out of the joint.

Roselli didn't check out of his room at the run-down hotel off the boardwalk where dealers, bookies, and waitresses lived, and Delphine didn't check out of her room in a rooming house either. In her convertible in the lot behind Rocky's Royal Flush, she was waiting for Roselli.

Delphine had practically raised herself, so she could be forgiven for placing so high a value on her friendship with Sally Dugan that she had mentioned in a hush to Sally that she was leaving town. Sally was closer to her than a sister was to other women, or even a mother was. Anyway, she trusted Sally, who crossed her heart and hoped to die if she told a soul as she, Delphine, had done when Sally told her all about her johns, and her own dream of finding a guy who would lay a golden egg in *her* bed. Delphine wanted Sally not to give up hope now, since she herself had found one in Roselli.

As Roselli had also told her to do, following at least this instruction to the letter, Delphine stuffed her valuables in her purse and left everything else behind, all her clothes, her furniture, which was nicer than what came with the room otherwise, and had even left behind her electric guitar, which she practiced with, earning her living in a casino show in a threesome, backup singers for a very-big-name canary. When that canary's gig was up, Delphine could always find work with another singer or orchestra, always in the background, but always so unearthly pretty that just to have her there made the musicians play better, and made the customers sit up straight.

Leaving without suitcases prevented early alarms from going off in Jimmy's office and in Reno's bar. Beginning the day before he took in the bets, Roselli knew he had been watched. Crouched down now, he sneaked out Rocky's back door and crawled into Delphine's convertible on his hands and knees. Slumped way down in the seat, the packages of groceries were heaped on top of him by Delphine, who drove. Nice and easy she went. His face was down by her knees, where his nose was taking in the violet scent she squirted in her underpants. The radio was rocking so loud he could barely stay in touch with his fear. Then they were out of town, the sixth stoplight behind them. Then Roselli took the wheel.

In a little town on the sandy coast that had white and blue houses looking out on the ocean that was like a blue plate it seemed that flat in the afternoon, they stopped at a ritzy bed-and-breakfast. The next morning when the waves were crashing out on the shore, they sounded to Roselli like gunshots. The worry he had was webbed on his spine. After robbing Jimmy and Reno of half a million clams or, in their way of looking at it, of welshing on the bets they had placed with him, he knew he had put himself at the top of their wanted lists. They had meant to rob him by betting on a race they had fixed, so turn-about was fair play, except there was no such thing as fair play when it came to dealing with them. But Roselli was out of reach now, and after a while he and they would forget the money was ripped off and they would all come to believe it was rightfully his and Delphine's in the first place.

The bills were stacked on the TV when they moved into their own rented beach house the next night, using new names they found in the local phonebook. A striptease by Delphine had Roselli thinking he was in heaven, and she did a lot of other things that he didn't even have to ask for. The money on the TV was then taken by her and rubbed all over her skin that had a beautiful sheen to it, and she was as happy as one could be only a few times in a lifetime. Their two-story clapboard house was painted white and had a black roof that came to a peak, and around the house was a white picket fence, and the Atlantic was out back, and in the front was a lawn of fine grass with sprinklers to keep the grass green. To buy new wardrobes, they left the house for one long weekend in New York, where they also spent a bundle on jewelry for Delphine. A new car zipped them back to the tiny town on the coast. There they loved rubbing shoulders day and night, and Delphine found out that she was a pretty good cook after all.

In a few weeks fall arrived with a chilling wind that Roselli thought was whispering threats of storms to come, but the late-September sunlight was tamed of the bite it had in June on the boardwalk, and now, at last, Roselli had a lasting place in Delphine's bed. The antique bed of faded brass was *their* bed and it was gushed over by Delphine, who would have another just like it someday, he promised, when they would furnish their own house. The clock-radio would be set sometimes to get them up to witness the toasted sun popping up to paste childlike grins on their faces before they dozed off again. The morning or even the whole day might be used up under the covers, kiss for kiss matched in every way. If anything was left of them, he might later go out to mow the lawn in his gold chain and white mocs, and she might bake biscuits or write a poem. They thought they were living the average life which never was lived by those hanging around the casinos and bars, but even in that small vacation town, they were suspected of living secretly, and indolently, without jobs, like the rich and famous, especially when their good looks and fancy clothes were included in the surmises of the townsfolk. The usual summer visitors having taken their silly outfits back to the city left the locals in the town hungry for a topic of conversation. So they gossiped about the young couple seemingly on an extended honeymoon with the other beach houses around them unoccupied now.

Unimportant quarrels a few months later were due to the

unused time Roselli and Delphine had on their hands every day. Not working, not learning, not gardening, not traveling, they were irritated by being constantly around each other, putting on weight, watching ball games on TV which seemed like replays of other ball games, and falling asleep on the movies on cassettes. So then they talked about possibly staying in Brazil after going there early in the spring for the carnival, or getting married and raising babies in California. But travel would bore them, they agreed, and kids would test their nerves, which were already jumpy from years under the fluorescents, but they would get married because they knew they would always love each other and every young woman wanted to be a bride. The second thing they could probably do successfully was operate their own joint. Delphine could sing and strum her new electric guitar for the patrons while Roselli might book a few bets on the side.

A hundred grand was hard for Delphine to part with for the bar and liquor license in the city forty minutes further along the shore, but she finally agreed that it was a worthwhile investment. When Roselli went to negotiate with the agent, and Delphine was alone in the house, she phoned her best friend, Sally, to ask if Sally wanted to tend bar when the deal was final, and if she could be her maid of honor, and if she would consider settling down in the same little town, where she might find a husband herself someday.

The next morning the lock in their back door was quietly jimmied open by an old woman with a shopping bag stuffed with her knitting. Seated in their bedroom, the old woman's long fingers conducted the knitting needles in and out of the lavender wool while they still slept. The sudden awareness that something was wrong in the room propelled Roselli up from his pillow minutes later. The pearl-handled pistol instantly in the old woman's two steady hands pointed at his eyes, he thought.

"I could have shot the two of you, if I wanted to, while you were asleep. But Alice doesn't really want to if she doesn't have to," said the tall white-haired woman gently. A prettiness was still in her wrinkled face, a trimness and good posture in her figure, as if she might have once been a show girl, it crossed his mind. The gun didn't frighten him. The woman herself wasn't exactly a menacing figure, and she might be taken in by a good con, he thought. Anyway, hidden under his pillow for just such an emergency was his Beretta.

"If we can all have some coffee, we can make a lot more sense when we talk," said Roselli. "But first of all, I have to go to the john. It's what normal people do when they wake up."

Without asking why she was there the reason was clear to him, but he was mystified about how she had found them. Beside him Delphine was bug-eyed; and her beautifully manicured fingers encircled his forearm as she held on for dear life. The leak in their boat had come from her mouth, she knew—calling Sally had been a very serious boo-boo; she wouldn't ever do that again if she didn't get killed first. The important thing that her mouth couldn't say now was said instead by her eyes. The message that Roselli received and understood was—she was more scared than all the other times she had been scared put together, and he had to save her and himself.

"You can't move from the bed," said Alice. "Not until you tell me where the money is. You know Reno. He wants his money back. So does Jimmy. They said—If Roselli gives it back, all of it, then we can be friends, let bygones be bygones."

"There any chance we can work out some kind of arrangement, you and us? Suppose we split it and screw those guys?" Roselli flashed his smile, disobediently dropping his legs over the bedside, not yet reaching under his pillow. "I don't want to piss in my PJs, lady, have a heart."

"Go ahead, go to the toilet. I wouldn't want your girlfriend thinking you were that scared. But leave the door open, so I can see you every second. I wouldn't want you to do anything funny. I've seen a man pee lots of times." To put a shine on their dark thoughts, the old woman as a woman returned his smile, which was deceitful in this case for both of them. His teeth brushed too, Roselli then returned to sit on the bed to take Delphine's hands in his hands. Then he kissed her to reassure her. Then he gripped the Italian pistol and released the safety.

"So, Roselli, are you going to tell me where the money is?" said Alice, shifting her aim to Delphine. "Or, should I shoot her first? To convince you I have to have it? All of it, not for me, because I'm not greedy as you and Reno are, all of it because I have to bring it back. It's my job."

To show he was giving in, he hunched over and said, "It's outside in the lawn, under the flamingo. You want me to go out to get it for you? A big bundle ain't so important as we thought," said Roselli. "So that's fine, take it back, we can be just as happy without it."

"You wouldn't lie that it's under the flamingo," said Alice, stretching her neck to see out the window the pink plaster bird posed on one leg in the center of the lawn. "No, I don't think you would lie, because then, you know, I would have to plug you and your honey, and that's a waste when you don't have to die, if all you have to do is tell me the truth."

"It's the God's honest truth. The dough's under the flamingo. Just knock it over and you'll see it, like the bird laid a golden egg, and I'll gladly go out to get it even."

"It won't be necessary, I'll go get it myself," said Alice, keeping Roselli and Delphine at the opposite end of her pistol. "Now I want the both of you, and you mustn't be afraid, I just want to tie you up a little, to come over here. Then you won't be able to chase after me. I can't run in my old age with my arthritis. I want you to face the wall, and, oh yes, get down on your knees, please. I won't make the knot too tight, and you mustn't be afraid."

Not expecting a gun in Roselli's hands now, which intuition told her if he had had one it would have likely been brought into play by now, Alice was just a little less vigilant as Roselli and Delphine were complying with her instructions by getting out of bed.

Without time to aim carefully, knowing what kneeling against the wall meant, he just yanked the gun into the open while pulling the trigger at the same time. The remaining slugs in the Beretta were also about to be pumped into the old lady, but he wouldn't have to shoot again, even though she wasn't mortally wounded. Two shots missed but one had eaten into her right biceps, causing her to drop her gun, which was grabbed quickly by Delphine.

"Kill her, kill her," screamed Delphine.

"It ain't necessary," he said.

"She'll follow us wherever we go, for the rest of our lives. She'll never leave us in peace." Delphine waved around Alice's pistol with the pearl handles as if she might do it herself.

Back down in the chair she had been getting up from when she was shot, Alice said, "It won't be me looking for you the next time. Since I failed, Reno will send someone else, probably two guys. Those guys you should kill if you see them, but not me. All I was interested in was the money. I didn't have no hits in mind."

"That's bullshit," said Roselli. "I know how the game's played, but all the same, we ain't bumping you, even though you deserve it for working for that lowlife Reno, and coming here to do his dirty work."

"Well, I'll just leave now," said Alice, but she was waved down again by Roselli's Beretta.

"Tear a sheet up into strips," he said to Delphine. "We'll tie her up and she can stay here for a few days, until somebody comes by, while we get a running start. When she talks to Reno again, we'll be long gone, and he'll have to figure out where we went." He almost seemed to be enjoying that the cat would have to come looking again for the mice that got away. Now that he had survived Alice's visit the danger to come was nearly a challenge, something to keep him on his toes, keep him feisty.

Strips of cloth were made by Delphine's steady hands, and she said, "You're making a mistake, Roselli, not killing her. A woman loves to talk. Everybody on the boardwalk could be out looking for us to get their hands on the money. She even knows the car we drive, the license number."

"The next time we see her I'll plug her right between the eyes, okay? But not this time. We don't need no murder rap," he said. "Come on, Alice, kneel facing the wall as you were going to have us do." The strips were tied securely on her wrists behind her back and on her ankles, by Roselli, while Delphine trained the pistol on the back of her head. When he was done, Delphine tucked the pistol away in her purse.

The flamingo outside was knocked over by his foot and he picked up the case with the money. The ignition wires were ripped out from Alice's car, and then they got into their own car. Just before he turned the key, Delphine said, "Can you wait just a minute, honey? My period's giving me an awful cramp, and I think I'll just run back in for a minute to put the pills the doctor gave me in my purse. Watch our baby," she said, patting the money case on the seat. "I'll be right back."

"Can you make it quick?" he said.

NUMBER TEN FOR POTATOES

I'm rocking in a chair. It's really not a rocking chair. It's a big chair and a soft chair. It's too big to be a rocking chair but I'm rocking it anyway. It's in a living room with other big chairs and two sofas and lamps and tables. It's a room like in my father's house. My father is in a big chair. The other man is also in a big chair. They're talking in their big chairs while I'm rocking in mine.

"He'll be twenty-nine in March," my father says. "With Dolly gone, and me seventy-two, it's time to make plans. Still, another twenty years would be nice."

"We all hope for that," the other man says.

"But we never know," my father says, and laughs. It makes me laugh when my father laughs. So now I'm rocking and I'm laughing. "See how he is," my father says. They look at me. "He's a joy. Dolly was crazy about him. Rocky could never make the trouble I made. He can't even tell the smallest lie. Still, as you know yourself, it's a heartbreak."

"He's a nice-looking boy too," the other man says. "My Karen, over the holidays, put on a few pounds, with her sweet tooth." He gets up and comes over to my chair. "Karen's my daughter," he says to me. "Her mother's doing her hair. She has long blond hair and blue eyes. You're going to like Karen."

"I'm going to like Karen," I tell him. "And what's your name, mister?" I say.

"Good that you asked. You're pretty smart," he says. "My name's Philip Higgins. Call me Phil."

"My name's Rocky Boyle. Call me Rocky."

"Rocky, I'm pleased to meet you," Phil says, and we shake hands. Then he goes back to his big chair and talks to my father again. "I'd like to keep Karen here with me and my wife. But we're getting on too. I had surgery recently. So Dolores worries if we both suddenly go, Karen, despite the trust, might go to an institution." Now Phil smokes a pipe. My father used to smoke one. He showed me how to smoke it. So then we both smoked it. Then my mother told us to stop. So then we stopped. "Dolores thinks Karen has become smarter," Phil says to my father. "She has, in some ways." Now Phil blows out smoke. "Karen has seen how her mother makes this a comfortable home. So Dolores thinks, if Karen has someone to help out, she can have her own home."

"Your tie, Rocky," my father says, "it needs to go up." So then I push it up. "That's good," he says. To Phil, he says, "He's neat and clean around the house. Sometimes he shaves twice a day. And he's strong. I get him to open lids on bottles and jars for me."

"Damn tight, those lids," Phil says, and laughs now. Then

he comes over to me again, and says, "Rocky, my wife and daughter are on the stairs now. So you might want to stand up to shake hands, when they come in." So I look out the door. "There she is," he says. "Isn't she a pretty girl?"

Her head is down. So I can't see her so good. Maybe Karen spilled her milk. When I spilled mine, my mother used to cry, so I used to put my head down too.

"This is our daughter Karen Higgins," the lady says. "My name is Mrs. Higgins. We're pleased to meet you, Rocky. Please, Karen, pick your head up and say hello. Rocky came here just to meet you."

Then Karen picks her head up. So I say, "You're a pretty girl, Karen. You have big blue eyes and long blond hair." Then I take her hand. "You have a pretty dress." Then I say, "Do you want to shake hands?" Then we shake hands. "Do you want to kiss too?" I say. Karen hides her face in her mother's dress. Everybody laughs.

Mrs. Higgins holds Karen's hand as they sit on a sofa. "Come sit here with us," Mrs. Higgins says to me. So I go sit next to Karen. Her mother says to her, "Why don't you ask Rocky about his hobby, ask him, 'What's your hobby, Rocky?' "

Then Karen looks at me with a big smile and says, "What's your hobby, Rocky?"

"Well, I like to take care of dogs," I say. "People from around different places bring their dogs over to my yard. I give them a bath. I brush them. I take them for walks. And sometimes I throw a Frisbee and they catch it and bring it back."

"Tell Karen how much you make," my father says.

"A dollar," I say.

"It's more than that," he says.

"I forgot," I say.

"A hundred dollars a week," he says.

"Yes, a hundred dollars," I say, and laugh, and everybody laughs too.

"I like dogs too," Karen says. "And cats."

"Is dogs and cats your hobby?" I say to her.

"I have two hobbies," Karen says. "One is cooking with Mother. And one hobby is reading with Father."

"I can't read so good," I say.

"I can show you how," Karen says.

"I'd like that," I say.

"You can kiss me now," she says. Nobody laughs. Everybody is quiet. So when I kiss Karen on the cheek, it makes a big noise. "That's nice," she says. "Let's go for a walk in the garden. I'll show you my cat first. Her name is Tiger. She has kittens in the laundry room."

"I like cats," I say.

"Children, don't be gone too long," Mrs. Higgins says. "We'll have lunch soon, in the dining room." Mrs. Higgins looks at my father, and says, "They make a beautiful couple." Then she looks at Karen and me. "If it starts to rain—it looks like rain out there—be sure to come right in. Karen, I don't want you to have another cold."

"I won't have a cold," Karen says.

"We'll come back for lunch," I say. "What's for lunch?"

Before Mrs. Higgins says it, Karen says it. "Smoked salmon and cream cheese. I helped to get it all ready."

"It's wonderful, Karen, you helped to get it all ready," I say, as we go to the laundry room. An orange cat and naked kittens are on a pillow in a wood box next to the radiators. The kittens are tiny. Karen picks one up and puts it in my hand. It's warm and soft. I put it next to my cheek. Then I give it back to Karen. She puts it back with the mother cat. "These are wonderful kittens," I say.

"Let's go out to the garden," she says, and takes my hand. We go out the back door in the laundry room and walk on the grass. "My mother told me all about the birds and the bees," Karen says. "How they make baby birds and baby bees."

"How do they do that?" I say.

"They have to get married first," Karen says.

"I didn't know that."

"So, Rocky, will you marry me?"

"Sure, I'll marry you, Karen. Can I kiss you all the time then?"

"Mother says if we get married you can kiss me all the time," she says.

"It's wonderful to kiss you." I kiss her cheek again. "I could do it every minute."

"It's wonderful for me too. Do it again, Rocky."

So I kiss her again. Then I feel drops of water on my head. "Karen, it's raining."

"Yes, it's raining, Rocky. But I don't care."

"I don't care either if it's raining."

"Now it's raining pretty hard," she says.

"It's wonderful to run all around when it's raining pretty hard," I say. "Let's run all around, holding hands, and we'll get all wet."

"Okay." She runs with me, and we both laugh so hard we don't hear her father and my father. When we see them under the patio roof, we stop. Then we hear them. "I think they want us to come in," Karen says.

"It's wonderful out here in the rain," I say. "I think we'll stay out here instead."

"If you say so. But Rocky, my dress is pretty wet now."

"Then we'll have to go in," I say. "Anyway, I'm pretty hungry. Are you pretty hungry, Karen?"

"I'm very, very hungry," she says. So we run to the house.

After the wonderful sandwiches, we have chocolate fudge ice cream. Karen says it's her favorite. It's close to my favorite, chocolate chip ice cream. Then Karen says to me, "Is it okay if we tell them we're getting married?"

"Sure, it's okay."

So Karen looks at her mother and says, "We're getting married, Rocky and me."

They make big smiles. "That's lovely, dear," Mrs. Higgins says. "We'll have to see. We're delighted, of course, that you like each other. But it can't be decided so quickly."

"You understand, Karen and Rocky," her father says, "if you get married, you'll live together, sleep together, take care of each other."

"Can she live in the cottage with me?" I say. "It's where I take care of the dogs. Karen can help me with dogs. And I'll help her with her cat and kittens."

"The cottage might be a good place," my father says. "We have more than enough furniture." To Phil and Mrs. Higgins, he says, "There's a little guest cottage behind the main house. Rocky has a cot there. He stays there a few nights a week."

"Maybe they should just live together," Phil says. "See how it works out. What do you think, dear?"

"In time, yes," Mrs. Higgins says. "The first step, however, should be courtship. They should do things together, like food shopping, cooking, the business with the dogs, and play things, like dancing, rowing a boat on the Sound, and manage a little money together."

"We want to get married right away," Karen says. "So he can kiss me all the time."

"He can kiss you every time he sees you," Phil says. "I'm glad he wants to kiss you, Karen. You're going to be very happy together. Mother just wants to be sure it's more than infatuation, that you'll both care deeply, as Mother and I care deeply."

"On caring deeply, Rocky's way ahead of me," my father says. "He cares deeply about everyone, every living thing." Now my father blows me a kiss. So I blow one back. "Rocky's love is unconditional," he says. "He never worries about getting back as much as he gives, or about losing his pride. He just loves you, no questions asked, nothing expected. I wish I could be like that."

"My daughter too," Mrs. Higgins says.

Karen and me are not too sure what they're talking about. So I just move my chair closer to her chair. Then we hold hands on the table.

After my father and me go home, the next day, and almost every day, we go back to Phil and Mrs. Higgins's house, or they come over to my father's house. Every time Karen and me hold hands and kiss. We all go out to different places. Sometimes just Karen and me go out. Then she holds my arm before we cross a street. It's up to me to be sure the light is green before Karen on my arm crosses a street. Sometimes if it's raining very hard I don't see her. But we talk on the phone. When I see her we can't stop holding hands and kissing. So then everybody says we should get married right away. So Karen puts on a pretty white dress and a lot of people come to the party. Then she comes to live in the cottage. On the first night, because of the dogs, Karen's orange cat runs away. So Karen cries while I look for the cat under the trees in the dark. But I can't find it. So then Karen says, "I'll just get another cat, Rocky," and she stops crying.

"I'll get you a whole bunch of cats," I say. Then we sleep in a big bed and I hold her tight.

In the afternoon Phil and Mrs. Higgins come around. "I'll call you every morning, Karen, to remind you," Mrs. Higgins says, "to take the pill. I'll also call to remind you when not to take it."

We don't know what a honeymoon is. But they all say we don't need one now. Next summer, Karen's parents say, we'll go with them to see the Grand Canyon and Yellowstone. And it can be our honeymoon too. Phil flies his own plane, so we'll fly in his plane. Karen was already up in his plane. I've never been up in any plane. It must be wonderful. But now it's wonderful to be with Karen every day.

Before we got married my father said it would be okay to put my penis inside Karen like a dog does to a dog sometimes when I take care of them. Karen says her mother told her it was okay too. But Karen has to take a pill every morning so we don't make a baby. Mrs. Higgins and Phil and my father all say we shouldn't make a baby. So Karen takes a pill in the morning.

Once a week a taxi takes us to the supermarket. My father pays for the taxi. But we pay at the supermarket. Karen and me, all week, write down on a list what to buy. Sometimes we don't know the word, so we use a number instead. We know numbers up to a hundred. Number ten for potatoes. Number eleven for chocolate fudge ice cream. Number twelve for detergent. Karen cooks the food. And I wash the dishes. There is no dishwasher in the cottage like in the house where my father lives. My father misses my mother and likes to be where she used to be.

Also, once a week, a taxi takes us to the movies. I'm learning to call a taxi on the phone and pay the driver myself. I tell him to come back when the movie is over. Like my father says, I give him an extra dollar as a tip each time. Sometimes we take a bus too. But no bus goes from the cottage. From the cottage we take a taxi. We also go for walks together, and to buy shoes, and we brush dogs. Karen also takes care of cats when the owners have to go away. Her father, Phil, bought these nice big cages for the cats and built a fence around the cages so dogs can't bother the cats. The cats come out of the cages into little yards behind the cages to stretch out in the sunshine. I help Karen with cats. And we save some money we make in the bank and spend some on things we buy.

"You and Karen have a normal life now," my father says. "Hold on to it, Rocky. Try to let no one take it away." When my father sits in the big chair in the cottage, Karen and me sit on the sofa. He gave us the big chair and the sofa and everything. He comes a couple of times a week. He used to work in the bank. Now he fixes the sink, shows me how to fix other things, and my father and me paint the walls and ceilings in the cottage. "I might not always be here. So, Rocky, learn as much as you can," he says. "From Phil too when he comes around."

"If you won't always be here," I say, "where are you going, Daddy?"

"Well, nobody lives forever," he says. "If I'm not here, there's Phil, and Mrs. Higgins to lend a hand."

Phil is nice too. I like it when he comes to see us too. He sits in the big chair too and smokes his pipe. He tells us about different kinds of fish. He used to study all about different kinds of fish. But now he is retired and stays home or flies in his plane. When he comes to see us, he brings us doughnuts, a whole boxful. Then Karen makes coffee and we have coffee and doughnuts in the garden. "I can't tell you," Phil says, "what a pleasure it is to come here."

Mrs. Higgins is nice too. But when she comes to see us she makes Karen cry. "Mice droppings are all over your kitchen floor, Karen. Shame on you," she says. "It's because you don't sweep up all the crumbs, and forgot to mop the floor." Then she goes in our bedroom and looks in the drawers, and says, "You forgot to wash the dirty clothes again. No clean underwear anywhere. Shame on you, Karen." But I don't mind if Karen forgot. I forgot too. And I don't like that Mrs. Higgins makes Karen cry.

So I say, "I'm sorry, Mrs. Higgins, but you have to go away now to your own house. I don't want Karen to cry."

"Don't tell me what I can say to my own daughter," she says. "And you, Rocky, shame on you for letting all the dogs into this cottage. The place stinks terribly. It's full of dog hair, old bones, paw prints everywhere. They shouldn't be allowed inside."

"When it rains," I say, "I can't leave them outside."

"A home is for people," she says. "The yard for dogs."

"I'm sorry, Mrs. Higgins, but you have to go away. I don't want Karen to cry anymore." So then Mrs. Higgins sits down in the big chair. She doesn't go away. Karen is still crying. So then I pick Mrs. Higgins up in my arms like she is a puppy. And I carry her outside and put her down in the garden. Then she goes away very mad.

The next day Phil comes to see us. He brings a whole bunch

of corned beef and potato salad and cole slaw and rye bread. In the garden we have a picnic. Then Phil asks what happened when his wife came over. So I tell him what happened. He laughs and lights his pipe. "I'm happy to know that when Mrs. Higgins comes around, you won't allow her to make Karen cry," he said.

Phil takes Karen and me up in his plane. It's wonderful up in the air. We are like the wind flying around. We fly all around over the trees and the grass. It looks different down there when we are the wind up here. We look up at the clouds too. Then Phil says, "Look over there." So we look. "That's Hartford," he says. "It's a city where a lot of people live." Then we fly and fly and then he says, "Look over there." It's all blue over there. And he says, "It's Long Island Sound. See the boats down there?" We see the boats with white sails. "All life comes from the sea," he says. But we don't know what he means. "Isn't the water down there pretty?" he says.

A couple of days later Mrs. Higgins comes to the cottage and this time she is the one crying. So I have to hold her. When Karen also holds her, she stops crying. "Your father, Karen," Mrs. Higgins says, and cries again, "his plane crashed into the Sound. He died, Karen. He's gone." Then she cries and cries. And Karen cries. Then my father brings brandy to the cottage. Mrs. Higgins sips the brandy, and says to my father, "He refused to go back to the hospital."

"I'm awfully sorry," my father says. "I liked Phil a lot. We saw eye to eye."

"Will you help me with the arrangements?" Mrs. Higgins says. "Some divers found the wreckage. He was still inside."

First, Mrs. Higgins comes to see my father at his house.

Sometimes she comes every day. She forgets to see Karen and me. When she sees us she doesn't make Karen cry. She makes herself cry. So Karen and me hold her until she stops. Then another lady comes to see my father. Sometimes she comes every day. So Mrs. Higgins stops coming there. He says he needs to have a woman around. Not Mrs. Higgins. But Tina Louise. He says he likes Tina Louise, even though he is old and ugly, and she is young and pretty.

So then Mrs. Higgins comes to see us more and more. One day she says, "Karen, when was the last time you had your period?"

"I don't remember," Karen says.

"Your belly's getting terribly big. Did you forget to take the pill? Even after I called, and reminded you?"

"Maybe," Karen says.

"My God. I hope you're not pregnant."

"Pregnant?" Karen says. It's a word she doesn't know.

I know it. An owner says it about his dog sometimes. It means a dog is going to have puppies. But Karen can't have puppies.

"Damn, damn," Mrs. Higgins says. "Tomorrow, Karen, you're going to the doctor."

Karen is five months pregnant, her mother says. It's too late for an abortion, her mother says. A test shows it's a normal baby, her mother says. So we're going to have a baby in four months. Karen is so happy. I'm so happy. We love babies. We love puppies and kittens and bird babies and now we are going to have a baby.

"Children, I'm sorry to say—but you won't be able to keep the baby," Mrs. Higgins says. "You can't keep a clean house.

You have dogs in all the rooms. It isn't a healthy environment." Then Karen cries again. "You won't be able to teach it things it needs to know. You have no concept of what's foolish and what's sensible in life."

So then I pick Mrs. Higgins up in my arms. I carry her out to the garden. She comes back later with a policeman. He takes me to jail. My father comes to jail with Karen, who went to get him. He says to the policeman that I didn't hurt Mrs. Higgins. That I just carried her in my arms like she was a puppy. The policeman says I can go home. He says I can't carry Mrs. Higgins in my arms anymore. But I say to him maybe I'll still carry her. Even if he has to put me in jail again. If she makes Karen cry again.

Mrs. Higgins brings us fruits and vegetables, milk, and cheese, whole wheat bread, and fresh fish. She also gives Karen vitamin pills. And takes her to the doctor.

"I'm going to the doctor with Karen," I say, "because I miss her when she goes away." The doctor shakes my hand. "Rocky," he says, "it looks like you'll soon be the father of a baby girl."

It's wonderful when the baby girl is born. We name her Dolly after my mother. It's a wonderful baby girl. It's normal and healthy. Karen loves the baby. She feeds the baby at her breast. I take the baby for walks in the garden. The baby, just like Karen, has big blue eyes and blond hair. My father comes over with Tina Louise. They bring the baby lots of dolls and toys and dresses.

Then Mrs. Higgins brings a lady around from Child Welfare. Both ladies come every day. Sometimes they help to clean the cottage. One day Mrs. Higgins throws out all the food in the refrigerator. "It's all spoiled," she says. Then she goes to the store and buys things Karen and me don't like too much. Jars of food for Dolly. The baby likes Karen's milk. We also give her some hot dog and pork chop and pizza, banana and a little doughnut.

"I don't know what I can do to prevent it," my father says. "The agency wants a court order to take the baby." Karen cries. So I hold her. "I'll testify you two are the most gentle parents I've ever known," my father says. "How much that counts, I don't know. Maybe it's more important the floor is swept, that you read the classics."

We all go to the court. I sit with Karen at a table. A nice lady there says she is the lawyer. We don't know what that means. Me and Karen get up to answer questions in another chair. Then we come back to the table. Then my father and Tina Louise wipe their eyes. He says we lost the baby. I don't think so. I whisper to Karen that we will make another baby. And call her Dolly too. Then Dolly will be back in our cottage again. So Karen smiles now. She takes my hand and we go out of the court.

THE HANGMAN

On a dark, drippy Thursday morning, January 23, 1952, the *Sergeant Matsuko* tied up in Yokohama Harbor. It was named after a GI killed in World War II. Aboard were five hundred enlisted men and officers who sat in the drizzle, their butts to the steel decking, their ponchos like pup tents on their shoulders. They waited there like that for six hours, then off-loaded and boarded a train, which clanked along for another six hours. Then they boarded buses and finally arrived at Camp Drake.

Infantry, calvary, medical, clerical, culinary, all went through the same routine: fresh shots; films on how to stay dry in snowy Korea, how to use a pro kit before and after sex, and how to care for weapons. They also went to lectures on why they were there to fight, and how to survive under fire. They were issued woolens, extra socks, and a ration card for smokes and soap.

"This morning, men," Sergeant Bower said—his voice was loud enough without a PA—"we go get weapons. Noncoms get carbines. Privates get M-1s." Sergeant Bower had six stripes. His body was big. His face was big. He spat big in the dirt. And had a big southern accent. Sometimes he was likable, not often. "When we get back," he went on, "you all clean the Cosmoline, like it's gold, out of your weapons." The grease kept the rust off, but was a pain itself to clean off. If a speck of Cosmoline or lint was left behind from a swatch reamed into the barrel, an inspecting officer often became hysterical. "Then we go fire our weapons at the range," Sergeant Bower said. "If you do good, and if the captain's in a good mood, you'll get a pass to Tokyo. Any questions?"

To that usual question came the usual answer, shouted from the ranks—"Yeah, Sergeant—When do we eat?"

Neil Lonigan stepped out of ranks. "Sergeant Bower," he said, mouth dusty like the dirt underfoot, "according to the 1929 Geneva Convention, a medic can't carry a weapon. I'm a medic."

"Corporal," the sergeant said, and rolled like a tank toward Neil, "get back in the line. You take a weapon, you understand me?"

Neil decided to be nasty himself. "Sergeant," he said, "stick it up your ass." No matter how nice Neil would be, the sergeant wouldn't be won over. The sergeant followed orders and expected Neil to follow orders. So Neil wanted to be turned over to someone else who might listen.

"You little shithead . . ." the sergeant said, and whistled to a pair of three-stripe sergeants, who came running. "March this little turd to Captain Singleton's office, double-time. Corporal, you hear, double fucking time."

In the clerk's office, the sergeants at his side, Neil Lonigan stood at attention. They all waited for the captain to arrive in the next office. Two hours later the company clerk arrived. A sergeant explained why Neil was there. The clerk asked Neil about himself, then said, "I'm a draftee too, from Queens, Patrick O'Leary." They shook hands. After ten minutes the captain arrived. Neil was marched in.

"Two months ago," the captain said, "another medic, a corporal like you, Lonigan, refused a weapon. The first time he crawled out of a foxhole, a single round caught him between the eyes. Because of his armband, he was picked out in the dark. The only one killed," he said. "Son, I don't want you to get killed in Korea."

"Sir." Neil saluted, said, "I don't give a fuck."

The captain winced, and didn't return the uncalled-for salute. "You'll change your tune, soldier, when your ass gets court-martialed." He shouted, "Patrick O'Leary." The clerk came in. "Draw up special papers on this medic," the captain said. "We found him with Carmona's wallet." Baby-faced, roly-poly, and twinkle-eyed, the captain was also a liar and a bully. He said to the sergeants, "Throw him in the stockade. Tell McClusky's this one's a fairy." He winked at Neil. "Sergeant McClusky's hot for a fairy."

"Hey, Captain, wait a minute," Neil said, sweat on his brow. "Let's stick to the facts."

"Fuck the facts," the captain said. "You want to lose your ass in Korea. I'm going to court-martial it first here in Japan."

"Sir, you make a carbine sound pretty good," Neil said. "But stick it up your ass too."

"You see this dogface dies from exhaustion," the captain said to the sergeants. "Patrick," he said to the clerk, "also charge him with insubordination, failure to follow a legal order, and resisting arrest. We'll lock him up for twenty years."

Neil said, "Patrick, I can type up my own papers." It might, he thought, slightly endear him to the captain. "I used to help out in the office." It was a lie to postpone going to the stockade, but he knew how to type.

"Captain, I can sure use the help," the clerk said. "On the other five, the papers still aren't done yet."

"Sure, let him do his. It's like digging your own grave, before you're shot. But, general papers now."

On an old Remington Neil charged himself with crimes he hadn't committed. The papers were finished near dinnertime. He was marched off to the stockade. There his head was shaved down to the bare skin by Sergeant McClusky, who covered Neil's scalp with kisses. In his cell Neil had hard bread and three beans in a watery soup. Then he was marched to the mess kitchen, where he washed thousands of dinner trays. It was dawn the next morning when he was done. Before any sleep, unwashed and unshaved, he was marched back to the captain between guards with .45 side arms.

"Did you say," the captain said, "you'd rather have a .45, soldier?"

"No, sir," Neil said, exhausted. "No .45 either."

He was marched back again the following morning. In three days he had slept four hours. This time an M-1 was offered.

"No, sir," he said again.

Still again he was marched back the fourth morning. He sagged, thought he should give in, take the carbine, the hell with the Geneva Convention.

"Your orders came out," the captain said. "The evac hospital in Pusan."

"You can't keep me in the stockade," Neil said, dead on his feet, "without a hearing, Captain."

"I see you're miserable." The captain was pleased. "Well, you have some choices. Stay in the stockade. Go to Pusan with a weapon. Or type court-martial papers here. Patrick's going home."

"Sir, I'd be happy to be the clerk here," Neil said, straightened up. "Yes, sir. I would, sir." He saluted, and again wasn't saluted back.

"You'll be issued a weapon, as the clerk here," the captain said.

"Yes, sir," Neil said.

"What weapon do you want?"

"Sir, a carbine, and a .45 too."

"If another medic won't carry a weapon," Captain Singleton said, "I expect you to type up the papers."

"Yes, sir. I'll do that, sir," Neil said.

"Cut that out," the captain said. "Report to Sergeant Carmona."

Sergeant Mendes Carmona sounded like a mangy mongrel when he spoke normally. "I don't give no shit what you learn at Fort Jackson. Here you forget it." He had the face of a mongrel too. Five rows of fruit salad (ribbons like memorials for those he had shot on battlefields) were on his shirt. His back was as stiff as an officer's riding crop. "Here you do everything the way I say." His face growled at Neil. "Corporal, you look sloppy dressed. I hate that."

"I hate spit-and-polish," Neil told him.

"This is the fucking army," Mendes said. "This is your fucking sergeant talking to you."

"You're my fucking sergeant," Neil said.

"Maybe you go by plane to the front lines," Mendes said.

"Sergeant, I love spit-and-polish."

"You little mick," he said. "I got you."

Mendes was the company's top sergeant. He was always pissed off, without a good reason, regardless of how great things were for him. Every night he had his beautiful Michiko Yamamoto with him in bed. But not much was right with the world, he said, or with anyone in it, so it wasted his time to be nice, even to himself.

In their Japan Logistical Command Company, aka Japanese Lovers' Club, JLC on their shoulder patches, there were three officers and fifteen enlisted. The other draftees, besides Neil when he became clerk, were the mail clerk, Arthur Carrick, also a corporal, hometown Phoenix, and the second-in-command, First Lieutenant Roger E. Briggs, the son of a governor, once assigned to the First Calvary (tanks for horses). The First Calvary was fighting in Korea, where he couldn't be sent. He was the only officer on camp to carry around a riding crop. The captain and the second lieutenant and the other enlisted were all RAs, thirty-year men. Most had a wife and kids in the states, and some, like Neil, had a fiancée. Mendes had neither wife nor kids nor fiancée in the states, nor family anywhere. Except for Michiko, he was alone in the world. An outsider from an uncommon culture, once too poor, and possibly always too raw.

In his car, Mendes showed off his "moose." She sat almost under the steering wheel with him. They drove around like that in his red Chevy convertible. It had been shipped over at army expense. Most RAs in the JLC Company also kept a Japanese "wife" or girlfriend in a shack in Asaka, the village outside the front gates. A shack was usually one American room divided into four Japanese rooms and called a rabbit hutch by GIs. Mendes, at thirty-nine, barked at everyone, except the captain. It was pointless to punch Mendes in his big mouth. His bark was him, it came up from his soul. Higher-ups, also a little afraid of him, got out of his way. When possible, he was ignored, and wasn't invited along for brawls in Tokyo. Only Captain Singleton smiled on Mendes. Disliked by others, they liked each other.

After incoming GIs were processed on camp they were shipped out, usually, it seemed, at three in the morning. It usually drizzled too. And some GIs usually were AWOL. The gloom at that hour was lighted by truck headlights, which cast long shadows. The air was smoky with truck exhaust, with nearly everyone smoking, and with fog. The AWOLs had extended for themselves their passes to Tokyo. It usually turned out that they weren't AWOL. They were passed out drunk in a prostitute's shack, or flat broke without bus fare back, or lost and wanted to stay lost on streets in a language they couldn't read.

"You don't put them down AWOL," Mendes said to Neil. "When I get my hands on them, I strangle them."

The status of troops, incoming and permanent, in the JLC Company was reported every morning on a printed form. Numbers were filled in to show how many were on pass, furlough, temporary transfer, sick call, in the hospital, morgue, stockade, AWOL, and present and accounted for. So Neil reported AWOLs as sick calls.

They drifted back, or were hauled back by MPs, or were

turned in by prostitutes when dollars ran out. White and black AWOLs didn't blend in in Japan, and they weren't strangled by Mendes, or court-martialed by the captain. They were, instead, put on a nonstop flight to Korea. They arrived where the fighting was at the front lines sooner than if they had gone by ship from Sasebo.

Mendes, in the summer, became sick, but wouldn't say in what way. Neil suspected a case of syphilis. He knew that gonorrhea was curable. The mail clerk said he had been cured of gonorrhea three separate times. Or Mendes maybe had a case of worms.

Many Japanese, and some GIs too, according to medical lectures, had worms, because human waste was used to fertilize the crops of rice and vegetables growing in Japan's fields. It was collected house to house in wood barrels, called honey buckets, pulled in a wood cart by an ox or two. Human waste produced vegetables three to four times larger than nonorganic fertilizers, but harbored the larvae of worms. Tomatoes, carrots, and cabbages were sold from lean-tos by the side of the road and were bought by "mooses," who served the vegetables to their GI boyfriends. At the lectures the doctors showed the worms like ropes of raw sausages in mason jars.

Before Mendes left for the hospital, he said, "She's too ugly for me. So you have to do it, corporal."

"Christ," Neil protested. "Not me."

"First, she likes you more. Second, her husband deserves it. And third, I'm your fucking sergeant."

Bertha, Briggs's wife—they lived on camp in a small Cape Cod—often came to the dayroom in the barracks. She would put her feet up on the edge of the pool table when Neil and

Mendes played. It might be when Briggs was at the range. He went there every day to squeeze off a hundred rounds. Bertha herself wanted to be squeezed. So it was up to Neil now.

"Sergeant, if I get caught with Bertha," Neil said, "it might mean the firing squad for me."

"You have to do it," Sergeant Carmona said.

It wasn't such a bad idea, someone had to, but Mendes was sick. Most enlisted RAs thought it was SOP to keep hands off officers' wives. Bertha wasn't really ugly. She was really a looker, with dark eyes and dark hair. Neil, however, was crazy about Kazuko Okabashi. The first time he met Kazuko was on a bus to Tokyo. "Hello, soldier. How are you?" she said, in perfect English. They talked all the way in. Later, she said that she had grown up in Korea when Japan occupied Korea. Her father, a Japanese official, moved the family to Hiroshima. The bomb took her parents and brother. Kazuko, on the day it fell, was on a school outing on the city outskirts. Still, on her legs a few scars were like thumbprints. She was twenty-four, a year older than Neil. She also spoke French, Italian, and German. She taught him a little Japanese and Korean. She said her languages gave her the possibility of new families. They were almost never quiet together, and sometimes changed languages in the middle of a sentence. She worked for the army as the general's personal interpreter, and also lived in a barracks for Japanese women. Each barracks was an acre big, two stories of brown wood inside and outside, ballrooms with hundreds of bunks downstairs, small rooms upstairs where Japanese enlisted and officers had once lived themselves.

Neil took Kazuko to dinner at the Noncoms' Club, where she played the piano. "China Nights" made them moony. Her features were small and dainty. She made herself up sometimes with white cheeks like cherry blossoms, mouth red like cherries, and eyes lined in dark pencil, and looked like a doll in a glass case. In a silk kimono, Kazuko danced for Neil in a miniature room in a miniature hotel, in a village which seemed imaginary. One night she said, "If you ever go away, Neil, I will die. So you must stay here, and never go home."

It seemed an intense vow of love, but he had heard that other GIs were stabbed to death while they slept beside a Japanese girlfriend, who then stabbed herself. It happened about once a month when homebound orders came out. The GI packed up, and denied he had ever promised to take his girlfriend home too. So she stabbed them both.

A GI's Japanese girlfriend wasn't usually a prostitute. She worked in a shop or office, or went to college, and was seduced when a GI brought her mums and cordial cherries. He thought he was Romeo. She thought she was Madame Butterfly. It was romantic attention a girl didn't usually get from a Japanese suitor.

A girlfriend then often imagined herself as a GI bride. To improve her chances, she might have an eyelid operation at a clinic in Tokyo. She wanted round eyes like an American girl, but was often thought to be exotic because of her slanted eyes. So her operation usually disappointed her GI. Regardless of her eyes, she was left behind in most cases. Then she was despised by her family and community, and little hope was left of marrying a Japanese man.

Neil saw Kazuko almost every day, so he wasn't going to find it easy to get to Bertha. The idea, anyway, seemed more fun to think about than to do. It was risky, so maybe he wouldn't do it, but would claim, when Mendes came back, that he had.

Then Kazuko called to say that she was ill, and asked if he could bring her rice cakes. He gladly did. In her own tiny barracks room she doubled over, and sent him off. That evening he went to the dayroom, where Briggs and Bertha were shooting pool. To make a shot, Bertha leaned over, and underneath she had nothing on. It was an off-the-cushion shot which dropped the ball in the pocket. Still, she lost. Briggs stood his cue stick up in the wall rack. Bertha held on to hers, turned to Neil, said, "Corporal, do you want to rack them up?"

Neil's eyes sought Briggs's permission. "Go ahead," Briggs said, "play a game," and put his peaked cap on squarely. Then he switched his boot with his riding crop. It seemed to get his legs moving. "I'm OD this evening," he said, moving to the door. "It's time to make the rounds."

The officer of the day was in charge in the captain's absence. The captain was absent a lot. Whenever he came in, it was only for a few hours. The captain had a "wife" and kid in Asaka, another wife and kid in Minneapolis. He left Mendes to run things. While Mendes was absent, Neil was to run things. A lieutenant was always around for Neil to consult, for papers to be signed, and to talk to officers on the phone.

Neil racked up, won the toss, and broke the balls with the cue ball. Four and nine dropped into pockets. He shot again, eleven dropped in, and missed his third shot. It was Bertha's turn. She didn't take it. She locked the door, pushed the other balls in pockets, then lay back on the table, her skirt up. Neither spoke. Neil rolled up his pants and shirt and placed them under his knees, so neither his knees nor the green felt would rub off. Later he racked up again. This time Bertha broke the balls. Her first shot also sank two. They played rotation pool and she won.

Mendes came back from the hospital with his voice hoarser still, a gauze bandage over his windpipe. "The doctor says I always got a voice like this because in there is a tumor," he said. "Then it gets to be cancer. But now he takes it out. So now I'm okay," he said.

"You ought to take a vacation," Neil said. "I'll hold down the fort."

"You screwed up everything, Corporal, while I was gone. I looked over the papers. It's a mess." Mendes was glad to be pissed off again.

"You look like hell," Neil said. "You need some R&R." Rest and recreation, Neil thought, cured almost anything, but not, he knew, what ailed Mendes.

"If you didn't make Bertha, you're in deep shit," the sergeant said. Then he came back to Neil's suggestion, said, "Maybe, in two weeks, me and Michiko, we drive to Fujiyama."

The mountain, at least fifty miles away, seemed to rise up in the camp on clear days. The troops there would stand around to look at it as if it was God. The peak, even on a hot summer day, always had a white dunce cap on, as if God was also an incurable dummy. On an overcast day, it completely disappeared, seemed never to have been there in the first place.

"I didn't make her," Neil said.

"Yeah, you did. You and me, we got ice in our veins. We're the kind who could," the sergeant said.

"It's the truth," Neil insisted. "I didn't do it."

"Corporal, it's in your voice. It's like my voice."

Mendes's voice, Neil thought, wasn't like his. He was sure it wasn't, but he didn't argue. Mendes filled in a furlough form with Neil's name and signed the captain's name. It was Neil's reward. So he called Kazuko, and she was able to get a week's furlough too.

They went to stay at the base of Fujiyama. Outside their ancient inn a Buddhist monk struck a huge bronze gong a dozen times a day for reasons Neil didn't understand. The voice of the gong raised hairs at the back of Neil's head. That week with Kazuko was the sweetest time he ever had with a woman. Still, all their languages couldn't explain them to each other. It was what they wanted. Neil still received perfumed letters from his fiancée, Kathleen. Kathleen's snapshot mysteriously disappeared from his wallet. It was a load off his mind.

Mendes returned from his own leave, said, "It's time I get married to Michiko." He looked much better. "Then, maybe, we go home and have some kids."

He could write his own ticket, go to any U.S. Army base in the world, do any job or no job at all, salute or not salute an officer, sleep in his sack all day, and get drunk and swing at an MP. No matter how bad he was, he wasn't disciplined by an officer.

He sometimes spoke to Neil like a father, but didn't reform himself. He gave Michiko a black eye and split her lips. Gossip had reached him that while he was in the hospital Michiko had taken Briggs on a private tour of Tokyo. Bertha had pretended to be sick. She then opened the floodgates. Bertha's corruption had been fostered by Mendes. It then also fostered Michiko's corruption.

Kazuko, Neil hoped, wouldn't for his own part also be corrupted. She wasn't. She had other plans, one that failed, and another that succeeded. Kazuko stepped off the sidewalk in downtown Tokyo and walked straight into the taxi stampede on the Ginza when Neil's first homebound orders came out. Neil ran after her. Cars knocked them both to the pavement. Bleeding and bruised, they spent a week in the main hospital. By then his orders to go home were canceled. The second time his homebound orders came out they were canceled the next day, and canceled three more times after that. His frantic calls to headquarters were ignored. He stayed in Japan months after he was supposed to go home.

Mendes said he was tired of seeing Briggs and Bertha in the dayroom every night. They made him sick. He would just shoot them and be done with it. It wasn't taken lightly. Their dead bodies would cause problems for Captain Singleton. He hated even small problems like water marks on the windows. So the captain asked Neil to have a word with Kazuko. Her phone call from the general's office put Briggs and Bertha on a plane home.

In the winter, Mendes was to go back in the hospital. He wanted Neil and Kazuko to go out with him and Michiko first. He knew of a Tokyo restaurant where U.S. porterhouse was diverted from the officers' mess. He wouldn't say which officers were in the black market. Mendes, too, was in it. He bought hundreds of Lucky and Camel cartons at a buck each and sold them for two bucks to ready buyers bunched up outside the camp gates. Cigarettes were bought cheap only at the PX, and only with a ration card. The cards were kept by Neil under lock and key in the office, each good for two cartons when stamped. The captain kept his signature stamp also under lock and key. Mendes had duplicate keys.

The black market seemed too risky for Neil. Some GIs were arrested and flown to the front lines. Now Mendes proposed buying a dance hall in Asaka, to be stocked with pretty girls.

He had the cash. If Neil managed the place, nights and weekends, he would get half interest. To discuss the deal, and to drown the worry Mendes had about his upcoming hospital visit, they would go out on a Saturday night. They put on civies. Michiko and Kazuko put on silk kimonos. The night was freezing, but they rode in the red Chevy with the top down into Tokyo and on the Ginza, and took along a case of pink champagne packed with dry ice, two bits a bottle at the PX.

"In Portugal, my father catches the anchovies," Mendes said at dinner when they were a little light-headed. "When my mother dies, he takes me and my sister to Providence. He gets married again. His new wife wants her own babies. So, little by little, she kicks me out, my sister too. For a while, we live on the street. One night, my sister, she's fourteen, goes with a soldier, and doesn't come back. I'm fifteen, and winter's coming. It gets cold as a witch's tit in Providence. I lie about my age, and join the army, to have a warm bed. It's 1928."

Mendes ordered Japanese candy, sweet hard balls also somehow made from rice. They kept his mouth from going dry. He poured more champagne for all of them, drank his, and refilled his glass. He was getting drunk.

"After I come to Japan, the army wants volunteers to be the hangman. Me and five other sergeants go back to Leavenworth to study how a gallows gets built, and get the plans to build one—how high, how many steps up—thirteen. How to tie a rope in a noose, you make a S and then wind one end near one loop. And how to put the black hood on. Two sergeants, too dumb, get another assignment. Then General Walker of the Eighth Army—in charge of the executions—makes two teams. B team is the backup, in case something happens to us, if we get sick, or cold feet."

"Why," Neil said, "did you volunteer?"

"Somebody has to," Mendes said, "or they won't get hanged. They'd still be alive. We hanged them at Sugamo Prison, outside Tokyo. We start at midnight on December 23, 1948. Lined up first is Doihara, 'the Terror' of Manchuria; Matsui, 'the Raper' of Nanking; Tojo, the dictator; and Muto, of the Bataan Death March. The other sergeant in my A team puts on the hoods. He salutes the officer in charge and says everything is ready. The officer salutes back—that's the signal. Tojo and two others yell, 'Banzai,' then 'Dai Nippon,' or 'Japan is great.' I pull the handle. Then they all drop dead," Mendes said. "Corporal," he punched Neil's shoulder, "that's a joke, and you didn't laugh." So Neil faked a laugh. Mendes went on. "Under each one is a trapdoor. Four of them go together. Then we take them down. Then we hanged three more together."

The champagne was finished. Now Mendes started on sake. His tongue wasn't tripped up from all he had drunk. Every word, every pause seemed clear in his memory. He had to tell his story to willing listeners, to be passed down.

"They get told two hours before they get hanged. So then they clipped their fingernails, and cut off pieces of hair. It's a custom—am I right, Michiko, Kazuko?—the nails and hair go in the shrine where you worship your dead ancestors?"

Mendes didn't get an answer. He drank another sake, then took out his nail clipper and clipped his nails. The parings fell on a clean napkin on the table under his hands. Then he asked Michiko to cut some of his hair. She cut it at the back of his head with the nail clipper, and placed it on the parings. Mendes folded the napkin and handed it to Neil.

"Corporal, I don't know nobody else but you," Mendes said. It surprised Neil, who thought that Mendes knew hundreds of people. "I hope me and Michiko go back home. But if I don't come out of the hospital, she'll get some other GI," the sergeant said. "You just keep this napkin until you figure out something to do with it."

Neil put it in his inside pocket. Mendes was finally too drunk to stand up. So Neil drove them all back to camp. Two days later Mendes went to the hospital for more throat surgery. He left Neil in charge as before. Neil gave a headquarters sergeant five hundred stamped ration cards. The sergeant cut home-bound orders for Neil but promised not to publish them for forty-eight hours. Neil took off on a MATS four-engine, dented-aluminum-can-looking plane the next day. It was before Kazuko found out that he was on orders, and before she could stab him in the middle of the night. It was also before he heard how the surgery came out.

His plane refueled first on Wake Island. Then at Honolulu the GIs aboard got a six-hour pass to go to town. Neil got tanked up on beer in the Roast Pig Bar. When he came out of the john for the third time his sport jacket with Mendes's parings and clippings was missing. It had walked out of the bar on someone else's back. It didn't upset him. The jacket had seemed to him to be too heavy on his back anyway.

LOOSE CHANGE

I put one hand on my push-button knife in my pocket. Then I ask a guy who crosses to my side of the street, "Give me a hand, mister, will you?" The knife is in case he wants to steal from me. "I want to get this," I say, "up on the sidewalk."

It's a hand truck. It's piled up with shoulder pads, threads, buttons, zippers, and bindings. I pull it all to where I live with my mother. There it's all sewed into dresses.

"For a half-pint like you," the guy says, "this load's too big."

Now I pull the handles at the front, while he lifts the wheels at the back up from the street. Then he puts the wheels down on the sidewalk.

"Any chance, kid," he says, "you got a quarter?" He scratches his chin, which needs a shave. "I want to get some coffee," he says. He's pretty tall, pretty skinny too. His pants and shirt look too big, not too clean either.

I'm glad I don't need my knife. From my other pocket I take out my loose change—a quarter, two dimes, a nickel, and eight pennies. He doesn't actually want coffee. Anyhow I give him the change. This guy is old like my own papa. Papa used to be a janitor on Wall Street. Then his boss found some rum in his locker. So Papa got fired. Then he couldn't be a janitor nowhere else. So he went back to San Juan. He and Mama came here with Angel before I was born. Now, if Papa makes some money in San Juan, he sends it to us. It's never too much. And sometimes Mama has to send him some. When a new hotel gets built up in San Juan, Papa works as a carpenter.

"Thanks, kid," the guy says, and holds the change in his fist as if he doesn't trust his own pocket to hold it. "What's your name?" he says.

"It's David," I tell him.

"I'm glad to meet you, David," he says, and shakes my hand. "Tomorrow, David, I'll give you a hand with your truck again."

"Tomorrow it isn't shoulder pads," I tell him. "Tomorrow it's dresses. I have to take three racks of dresses to Prospect Avenue, at one o'clock."

"At one o'clock?" he says, figuring out what else he has to do at one o'clock.

"Maybe," I say, "I could use a hand."

"But I won't know," he says, "when it's one o'clock. I don't have a watch." He looks at my watch. "How about you lend me yours?"

"It's my father's watch," I tell him. "So I can't lend it to nobody. I promised my father."

It has a gold case, not real gold. And a leather strap, not real leather either. The best part is the Roman numbers.

"Lend me your watch," he says. "I'll give it back to you tomorrow."

He looks like a slob. So I don't know if I should lend it to him.

"I promise to give it back," he says. "And tomorrow, I'll give you a hand with the racks."

"Maybe you won't give it back," I say. I look at his belt. "You have to lend me something of yours too."

So he takes off his belt; and his pants droop. "I got this alligator belt at the Salvation Army," he says. "Some rich guy donated it." He hands it to me. Then he pulls up his pants. "It's the best thing I got."

I put the belt around my own pants. It has a gold buckle, probably not real gold. "You'll meet me here at one o'clock?" I ask him, and hand over my watch. "And what's your own name?"

"Felix," he says. "And tomorrow I'll be here at one o'clock. To give you a hand with the racks. I'll watch out that creeps, around Prospect Avenue, don't bother you, David."

"And tomorrow when I see you here," I say, "I'll give you your belt back. And you'll give me my watch back."

"I'll give it back," says Felix, and starts to go, then turns around to say, "Don't get a rupture pulling that thing." He laughs as he goes away.

It's loaded up to almost double over my head. It's not too heavy to pull in the street. Only to lift it up on the sidewalk it's too heavy. Mr. Sanchez orders all the fabrics and trimmings from the store. At the store, they are tied up tight with brown cord to keep them from falling off the truck. The truck fell over once, and all the boxes fell off. It took me an hour to tie them up again. So for an hour Mama and the ladies couldn't work.

They had to stay late to make it up. They get paid by the piece. For every shoulder pad they sew in a dress they get three cents. For every sleeve they get ten cents.

On two afternoons a week I cut school. On Thursday afternoon I pull fabrics and trimmings from the store to our rooms four blocks away. It takes two round trips, plus I bring back the empty truck. On Friday afternoon I pull the dresses they sew in a week over to Prospect Avenue. The ladies sew until they go home at night to their own rooms. Mostly they are mamas. One's a girl my own age who has Chinese eyes. Another's a black girl about a year older than me who cries a lot. When Mr. Sanchez comes around with the pay and his bodyguard, all the ladies each pay me a dollar. Mr. Sanchez first fixed up all the wires that go from the living room to Mama's bedroom and to Clara's bedroom. Then he moved in eight sewing machines. The ladies sit at the machines and sew and make farts from all the beans they eat; and even in summer nobody opens the windows.

If a window is open and the landlord Mr. K passes by, he'll find out sewing is going on. Then Mr. K could raise the rent, because it's illegal, Mama says, to have a dress factory in our rooms. Or Mr. K might call the health department. Then the health inspector has to be bribed. If he can't be bribed, and he shuts down the factory, then there's no work for the ladies. So the windows mostly stay closed up. After the ladies leave at night, Mama opens the windows. Then the rooms air out. If it's raining or snowing, the windows still stay closed up all night too.

Now I take my truck up the alley along the back of the buildings. The alley is piled up with garbage and mattresses. Slobs throw it out in the alley. Slobs don't care about anything, even if they live or die. We don't yell at them for throwing garbage out the back. They're like zombies who can't even wipe their asses. They easy get pretty wild. So I have a push-button knife with a four-inch blade in case a slob pulls one on me, or tries to steal from me. Around here if a guy doesn't fight back, he's dead meat. We all act like the slobs aren't here, which actually they aren't. Slobs, Angel says, have a bad case of the blues. He has it too. We all have some. Except, some get a bad case and take the medicine. Angel is smart, but he hated to make plastic holders for toilet paper, and plastic holders for paper towels, and he couldn't get any other job. So then he gets caught and goes to jail. Now I wish Angel was here to unload this stuff and carry it upstairs.

I always unload in the alley. And I take dresses out in the alley. If the landlord, Mr. K—he says his name is only the initial K but we don't believe him—happens to drive by he won't see it all. Twice a month Mr. K comes around to collect half a month's rent. People on the block can't save up a whole month's rent. He also drives by twice a week, he tells us, to see if his shitty tenants have totally destroyed his buildings. Mama and Jesus painted our own rooms blue and orange and white. But she doesn't let Mr. K. inside to see the fresh paint. Then he'll see all the sewing machines too.

The rent is split up by the ladies. The electric bill, too, is split up. It's what Mama gets out of it for letting our rooms turn into a dress factory—mostly free rent and mostly free electric.

Mr. K comes around in his gold car, probably not real gold, and I ask him what kind it is. "It's a German car," he says, and pats my head.

Like I'm four, he pats my head. Actually I'm fourteen. So I

get mad; and I go break an empty ketchup bottle on the curb. Under his back wheel I stick a jagged piece of glass and disguise it with paper trash. Then I disguise another jagged piece under his left front wheel. Then I watch him get in his car. I even wave. He never waves. He just starts up. He puts the car in drive, and he drives about six feet and stops. The back tire gets slashed good and goes flat. "David, can you find me someone," Mr. K says, getting out of his car, "to change the tire quickly?"

"Sure," I say, and I run down the block like I'm looking for someone, laughing all the way, and never asking any guy if he wants to change Mr. K's tire.

In the middle of the night something stinks when I go to the bathroom. Maybe the rooms still aren't aired out. So in the living room I open another window. I look down and see people asleep on the dark sidewalk. Then I go back to my room. It's also Angel's room; if he gets out on parole next month. I hope he stays on Rikers Island. He takes my money, my clean underwear, and never does anything for anybody. He actually can't. Now I have to get back to sleep. After I go to school tomorrow morning, I have to take the dresses to Prospect Avenue in the afternoon. I hope Felix shows up to give me a hand. I hope he doesn't think the watch is worth a fortune and doesn't show up.

The stink now gets pretty bad. It keeps me awake. I wonder if Mama, in her bedroom with Jesus, smells it too. I used to spit at Jesus. Then I had to stop when he didn't spit back. He's actually pretty nice. But I still won't call him by his name. Usually I say, "Hey, you." He's a guy who'll take any job. Since the beginning of time it could be the worst job. With one good eye, he doesn't get too many jobs. Once, when he was cleaning out some big vats, some acid splashed in his left eye, so now it's blind. Even if he's half blind, and never has any money hardly, Mama still likes him anyhow.

The stink gets very bad. So I have to get up from bed again. I decide to look in the kitchen. But the gas stove in the kitchen wasn't left on, which might make a stink. In the living room I flip the switch. The ceiling light doesn't turn on. Either the bulb burned out, or the fuse burned out. Fuses always burned out. Anyhow, in the dark it's easier to see the glow of a burning cushion. Jesus fell asleep watching TV, and maybe dropped his cigarette. So I look in the sofa and big chair. Nothing's burning. Only Clara's hairpins are under the cushions. Clara doesn't have any family of her own. So she rents a room from Mama. The stink must come from piled-up trash on the curb to be picked up tomorrow, Friday, as every Friday and Tuesday. In the trash something must be actually rotten.

On the way back to my room, Clara's door opens up. She comes out in the hall in her underwear. She's pretty old, about twenty-five. During the day she sleeps with guys in hallways. But at night she sleeps without guys in her bedroom. Mama won't allow guys in Clara's bedroom. So, once, Clara says to me, "At night, alone, I can't sleep so good. So maybe, David, you can keep me company." So a couple of times a week I keep her company. Sometimes we make out too. I'd also make out, if I could, with the girl with Chinese eyes. She's shy, and hardly says anything. When I talk to Soo Sin, Mama says, I have a funny look on my face, like I might get married to Soo Sin. But I won't get married to her.

Standing there half-naked, Clara coughs now a couple of times. So I say, "I think, Clara, you should have a glass of water. I'll get it for you." She shakes her head like she, too, can't hardly say anything like Soo Sin. Then she points to something in her room. I guess a guy is in there who sneaked in. When I go in, I see, instead, a bright light. And there the stink is the worst of anywhere.

Her light switch doesn't work either. Behind the two sewing machines on one side of her bed is a bright glow. Smoke goes up through the glow. It's the smoke that stinks so bad. So I open up her window. Then the glow bursts into flames. I slam the window closed again. Clara, out in the hall, screams, "Fire! Fire!" She shouldn't scream that. If firemen come here to put out a fire, they'll also put out all the sewing machines. Then Mama and the ladies will be out of work.

I don't know what to do first—smother the fire, or smother Clara. Right now the fire is more dangerous. So I throw Clara's pillows on the flames. I stomp on the pillows with my bare feet. Then I pull the burned wires apart. I don't touch where the insulation burned off, which Angel told me about. Angel told me about fuses too. Mama comes into the hall now and holds her hand over Clara's mouth. Then Jesus flies in with a pot of water. He dumps it on my feet. I could get electrocuted with the water and the bare wires. So I yell at Jesus, "Hey, you, stop that." He rushes out and comes back with another pot of water. Before he dumps it, I yell, "Jesus, it isn't necessary." Then he grins at me with his mouth of missing teeth.

The fire is out. But there's no electric. Even the refrigerator isn't going. So Mama gives me a flashlight and a fresh box of No. 30 fuses. In my pajamas I go downstairs and out the back door to the alley. Our fuse box is next to our meter, No. 3 for the third floor. All our fuses burned out. So now I unscrew one and pitch it across the alley at rats. Then I pitch another. On a pile of trash rats go up, down, and around. They go pretty fast. I don't get to hit any.

While I screw in new fuses, somebody from across the alley yells, "Hey, kid, c'mon over here. I'll give you some candy."

I don't see anybody. I see only another pile of trash on a rotten mattress. It turns out to be an old guy. He waves for me to come over. So I take out another new fuse from the package and pitch it at the old guy. It beans him right in the head. He yells. Then I go inside and up the stairs, which smell worse than a toilet that nobody since the beginning of time ever flushed.

In Clara's bedroom Jesus holds up the wires for me to see them. He's wrapped the bare copper ends in triple-size bandaids from Clara's dresser so the wires can't touch and short out again. "That's good, Jesus," I say. He grins at me again. He shouldn't ever grin at anybody. He has a big ugly grin. And Mama, I don't know how she does it, she sleeps with that big ugly grin every night. Now I go in the kitchen, where Mama is on the phone.

"My boy David put in new fuses," Mama says. "Mr. Sanchez, the lights work now, the other machines work now, but two machines still don't work. The two in Clara's room." She stops to listen. "If they don't work, the ladies on those machines don't work. They have to work, Mr. Sanchez. I'm sorry it's so early. I'm sorry I call you so early. But, please, you come right away to fix those machines." Now she listens again, then looks mad. "It's okay," she says, and doesn't sound mad. "Then today we ship you no dresses, none. We have almost finished three racks; only left to do is the hems." She waits, then, sweet as sugar, she says, "To do all the hems by one o'clock when David takes them to your truck, we need working eight machines. Now we have working only six machines." She listens. "Thank you, thank you, Mr. Sanchez," she says. "God bless you, Mr. Sanchez." After she hangs up, she says to me, "I put on that man, when I cut the chicken's throat, a curse. I ask for his blood to come out when he goes to the toilet and picks up the seat."

"You made a mistake about the hems," I say, as I thumb through dresses on a rack there in the kitchen. "These hems are all sewed."

"Yes. I make a mistake," she says. "Now, David, go take your shower. There's no more time to sleep. And I make you some eggs and coffee." In the hall she calls, "Jesus. Clara. Now we have the *cafe con leche.* In one hour Mr. Sanchez comes here to fix the machines."

Every morning Mama first sends me to take a shower. Then she sends Jesus to take a shower before he goes out to look for work. For a month at least he couldn't find any work. But last night he said he has some work today. He has to give out the new phone books. The company hires neighborhood guys because nobody else wants to come in here. His work is for only one week. And for only the minimum wage. This morning when he eats his eggs, he grins like mad. He didn't shave or take his shower yet, but already has on the clean shirt Mama ironed for him last night. After his shower usually comes Clara's shower. Last comes Mama's shower, if she has time. By then the water is always ice-cold. It's actually never hot. When I first turn it on, it acts like it's hot when a little hot comes out. Then it gets colder and colder. If the water's ice-cold in the summer, which now it's almost summer, I don't mind if it's ice-cold.

In the yard at Niles Williams JHS 118 this morning, kids stand around. Some brag, some smoke, some fight; some girls talk in a bunch; some girls jump rope; and some guys practice hoops. Most kids have their books and homework. Some always forget. In the yard, before the first bell, is where I do my homework. I do it pretty fast. A few kids in the yard sell dope. I sold it once myself, for about a week. Then I got beat up because I took customers away from another kid. I didn't want to get killed, or go to Rikers Island either, so I decided to go straight.

We call the homeroom teach by his first name because he has actually hard names—Joachim Onopnicka. Joachim says his people were poor too. But if we study hard, we'll get a good job later; then we won't be poor anymore. Another great teach is Mrs. Schwartz, who says I should go to college, and teach other neighborhood kids about science, like she does. But I think I'll collect rent like Mr. K does. Then I can have a German car, and live in Queens with a wife with red hair. He shows us pictures. His two kids also have red hair. Only he has white hair. Or maybe I'll be an engineer. Joachim says I should be an engineer. Maybe it's what I'll be, even though I'm not sure what an engineer does.

This morning Joachim says to me, "How come, David, you didn't do well on yesterday's test? You had three equations wrong." He hands me back the paper and waits for an answer.

"Three wrong out of twenty," I say, "isn't too bad."

"You usually," he says, "don't get any wrong."

Now I don't know what to tell him. I'm sorry he isn't too happy. So then I try to sound funny to cheer him up. "It's because," I say, "I'm in love with a girl with Chinese eyes." The other kids laugh. He doesn't.

"I see," he says. "Nonetheless, David, on your next test, I expect a hundred percent."

"She's awful pretty," I say.

"Is she Vietnamese?" he says.

"That's it," I say. "She's Vietnamese. Her name is Soo Sin."

"For your homework over the weekend, David," Joachim says, "solve the problems at the back of chapters eight and eleven, two chapters for you."

"Sure," I say. "I can easy do two chapters."

At lunch break today I go back home for lunch. Usually, at school, if I have any money, I buy lunch. If I haven't got any, then I ask cooks at school if I can have an orange for free, and sometimes I get an orange or a banana. Today Mama and me, we have cabbage and beans and tortillas for lunch. It's the day to take the dresses to the big trailer truck. Other kids, and some old guys, also pull dresses on racks in the streets from around the neighborhood. When we get to Prospect, Mr. Sanchez, at the back of the truck, will look over the dresses. He'll count them, write up a receipt, and write it down in his book. Then we take back three empty racks. The next day he comes to pay the ladies.

The hardest part is taking the racks down the stairs. Once, with just one full rack, I tried it alone. The rack got out of control. It rolled down one flight, and turned over. Some dresses got dirty on the stairs. So the ladies cleaned them up pretty fast so I could still get to the truck on time. Now all eight ladies and me, together, we take down the racks. On the stairs the ladies boss each other. They swear in Spanish. They say the racks are going to fall over any second. Sometimes they even shove, pinch, and punch each other. Usually they're not too mad. Usually they kid around about the guys they live with, about their kids, about the pains they have. A lady might say how her guy is out of work, or never cuts his toenails. Or, she might say how he screws her day and night and she can't wait to get home. Then the other ladies burst out laughing. Only one dress falls off today. Then they go back to sew on the machines again. Out in the alley, with two pieces of clothesline, I connect the racks one behind the other like the IRT. From the front I pull the racks down the alley out to the sidewalk where I'm supposed to meet Felix.

The second-hardest part is to let nobody steal any dresses. The racks are much heavier to pull than the hand truck loaded up with trimmings. But once the racks start rolling, it isn't hard to keep them rolling. I always have to keep an eye on the end rack. A slob, without me seeing him, could grab some dresses from the end rack. A slob will sell them for a fix. If a slob comes around my end rack, I get a little scared. Then I yell to people on the street to give me a hand. One old lady spun a trash-can cover like it was a Frisbee at a slob. Without it hitting him, the noise when it landed in the street scared him and he ran away. Twice, nobody was around to give me a hand. So I had to pop open the blade of my knife. The slobs got scared then, and ran away. I was pretty scared too.

Felix is waiting on the corner now. "Your watch," he says, "don't work so good, David. It runs for ten minutes, then it stops."

"Is that right?" I say. "I thought it works pretty good." I figured Felix would sell it for a half-pint. Then I'd keep his alligator belt. His belt works better than my watch. Now he gives me back my watch. So I give him back his belt. "Even though you didn't have the right time," I say, "I'm glad you showed up, Felix."

"What I had to do," he says, "is stay all morning near the big clock in the kitchen." Then he gets in front and pulls the racks.

"I haven't any money left," I say, from the back rack. "So I can't give you any change. Tomorrow, I'll get some."

"That's okay," Felix says. "At the Salvation Army, they want me to come back to help make supper."

"Can you take the racks to the back of the truck yourself?" I ask him. "While I take a leak?"

"Sure," Felix says. "Go ahead, David."

So he takes them to where Mr. Sanchez is standing on the tailgate. And I go to stand in front by the engine, unzip my fly, and look around. When nobody is watching me, I lift the hood up just enough to get my hands on the wires. I pull them out and cut them with my knife. Then I push the wires back in and close the hood again.

Then I go to the back of the truck where Mr. Sanchez is counting the dresses and Felix double-checks him. Mr. Sanchez finally hands me a receipt, and I say, "Thanks a lot. We'll be back here next week."

A MARVELOUS FEAT IN A COMMON PLACE

My cat wasn't much to look at and wasn't very polite either, having introduced herself the first time years ago when my apartment door had been left wide open on a hot summer day, coming inside from the trash barrels in the alley where she had lived up until then; but as a dead cat she looked instead like an apartment-size black panther, standing gracefully poised, alert and pretty, preserved with her white-sock feet firmly attached to a mahogany stand on the mantelpiece in my living room.

My cat Bast was stuffed and mounted for me by my upstairs neighbor in the apartment building, a butcher, after he'd shown me the stuffed sow that he keeps in his own apartment. That sow was the first that he ever slaughtered, he said, tears brimming from his eyes even now. To have my cat stuffed had cost me $385, raising a lot of doubt in my mind about having her preserved, but money was really of no importance in comparison to having my Bast back again. It was too late anyway, there she was, beautiful as she hadn't been in life; and I had to write out the check for the butcher, who was waiting with a meat cleaver in his hand.

Physical beauty, as far as I'm concerned, has very little appeal. I go to great lengths personally to be unattractive in order to discourage others from getting too close, not taking regular baths, shaves, or haircuts, eating ice cream and cookies to excess, all of which has built an invisible fence around me. Of course, Bast had more sense than to be concerned about my hygiene, hers none too fastidious either, so we had, as lovers say, found each other. She didn't interfere in the long quiet hours I spent on my treatise, and took unchallenged by me all the hours she spent prowling the streets at night. In the morning's first light we had both been delighted to meet again over her bowl of milk and dry cat food, and my bowl of apricots and granola.

Before Bast came into my life, I was content to work on my manuscript without conversation or the company of another living being, but after, my work went so much better than ever. When we had said "Meow" to each other, when she had curled up in my lap, sometimes sleeping with me in bed, Bast was like my muse, inspiring a new lyricism in my writing about the bedbug.

My lifelong ambition has been to write a definitive history of the bedbug over the millenniums, which I'm now doing, having taken a sabbatical from the university where I'm a professor of psychology. The *Cimex lectularius* is a bashful little thing which hates coming into the light where a vigilant sleeper might pick it off, and prefers of course its blood meal in the dark. Amazingly, it can live for as long as a year in an unoccupied bed on just the hope of a juicy behind getting in under the covers.

My thesis, which I intend to prove with historical research, is that the bedbug has shaped the world since before civilized times, making it what it is even today. For example, the bedbug, it might be said, has given birth to some of the most well known personalities through the ages when itching at night was commonly misinterpreted by men and women as raging carnal desire. In modern times there are instances that I point out in my book of the bedbug driving good and gentle souls to rise from their bed in the middle of the night for nefarious purposes.

My enthusiasm for the tiny creature, however, had waned ever since Bast didn't come back inside one morning two months ago. I went out to look for her, and my heart broke when I found her dead in the alley. Then I sat here in my big chair day and night gazing at my dear stuffed cat on the mantelpiece like an *objet d' art.* Petted or spoken to about astrophysics or Orchidaceae, other favorite subjects of our past conversations, Bast, glassy-eyed, had remained unresponsive until very early this morning. For the past few days I've been noticing that the level of dry food in the sack has been going down slowly. I suspected hungry mice, but this morning Bast smiles at me from the mantelpiece—which is outrageously wonderful—and tells me with her eyes that she's been the one nibbling on the dry cat food.

Her smile of course immediately brings my intense reaction—my humming of Mozart to her, which in our previous good times together she responded to with the motor in her throat. It's exactly what she's doing now, purring loudly as she first hesitates, then, crouching, jumps down from the mantelpiece in a wonderful high balletic leap right into my lap. "Bast, you've come back to life," I whisper, not wanting to frighten her with the shock of disbelief I feel but keep from my voice. As she always liked to do, Bast now rubs the top of her head on the point of my chin, then curls up contentedly.

It doesn't make an ounce of rational sense for a stuffed cat, despite the mythology of its nine lives, to be reincarnated before my astonished gaze. Am I imagining the impossible out of my grief for my deceased pet? Am I asleep and dreaming? I pinch myself and it hurts quite a lot, which doesn't really prove that I'm awake, but I assume so anyway. Now I look across at the mantelpiece and sure enough there is the wood stand which Bast was attached to, but it's vacant now. Bast isn't there. She's warm and gorgeous, not bony and threadbare as when she was alive the first time, and she curls up on my upper thighs as I sit in my chair. I'm forced to acknowledge that she has pulled off a marvelous feat in a common place, my living room.

Carrying Bast cradled like a baby in my arms, diamonds of light sprinkled on her glossy black coat, I go to the kitchen, where I gently set her down on the table to wait while I pour out a saucer of milk for her. Crouching down, she laps it up, understandably, like an animal who hasn't had a drink for quite a long while. "So, tell me, Bast," I say, my voice full of wonder, "how in the world did you accomplish this fantastic trick of coming to life again?"

Bast lifts her now pretty face to me, her yellow round eyes sending a message as if in digital zeros and ones, which my eyes, locking on to hers, can easily decode. Her explanation is simply that she now understands we are destined to be always together. And since I didn't also die to go where she was, she has had no other choice but to return to life, called back to be with me again by my deep sorrow at her passing.

Her eyes say that her death and departure occurred too abruptly through her own fault, always having been too impulsive, too quick to jump at things. With my own eyes I say to her that certainly she has pulled off something quite remarkable by coming alive again. But I have to remind her that she still can't speak with words, nor can she hum symphonic melodies, so we both still have to rely on our eyes and vocal sounds to communicate with each other.

The day just evaporates around us, Bast eager to hear what little progress I've made in my research and writing, and I ask about cat heaven, where, surprisingly, it turns out according to Bast that cats have to hunt down every meal they have as in the days before they came into our homes. When night falls now, Bast jumps down from my lap to the floor and pads to the apartment door, showing me the way she wants to go as before in her first life—whether to prowl in the night, sleep in bed, or look for something tasty to eat in the kitchen. Like most cat lovers, I think I've always understood her behavior, even as human behavior sometimes is very baffling to me. Tonight, however, I'm somewhat reluctant to allow her out of my sight after having been reunited for just twelve short hours. Still, the most one can do for a pet is to give it freedom to live a little of its life as it chooses, not enslaving the creature in exchange for a handful of food.

So I have to open the door for her, asking her plainly in my words and in my tone of voice to understand that I'd like her to come back as soon as possible. I'll leave the door ajar for her. When she comes in she can sleep in bed with me. She turns to give me what I think is a tender smile while also beckoning me with a nod of her head to follow her a little ways out of the apartment, regardless that, in my usual dress these last few months, I'm wearing soiled pajamas, buttons missing and held up with a safety pin.

Timidly, I take a few steps out of my apartment into the hallway and find by the wall a large brown box, the name of a pineapple juice company printed on the outside. Bast stops there and says "Meow" in a way which invites me to inspect the inside of this reused box, even though my name doesn't appear written on it. Sitting back on her haunches as if she knows well enough what I'll find, she waits to be praised and stroked. I turn back the corrugated box flaps and find inside two small weaned kittens, one white and one black, mewing and pawing a towel put down for their soft bed. "You're acting just like their mother, Bast," I say to her, "but you can't be." Bast accepts my petting on her head and coat, then wanders down the hallway and out of sight. When she doesn't come home that night, or the next morning, I have to weep for a few minutes, but then find new happiness with my kittens Pharaoh and Sphinx.

Short Story Index
1989-93

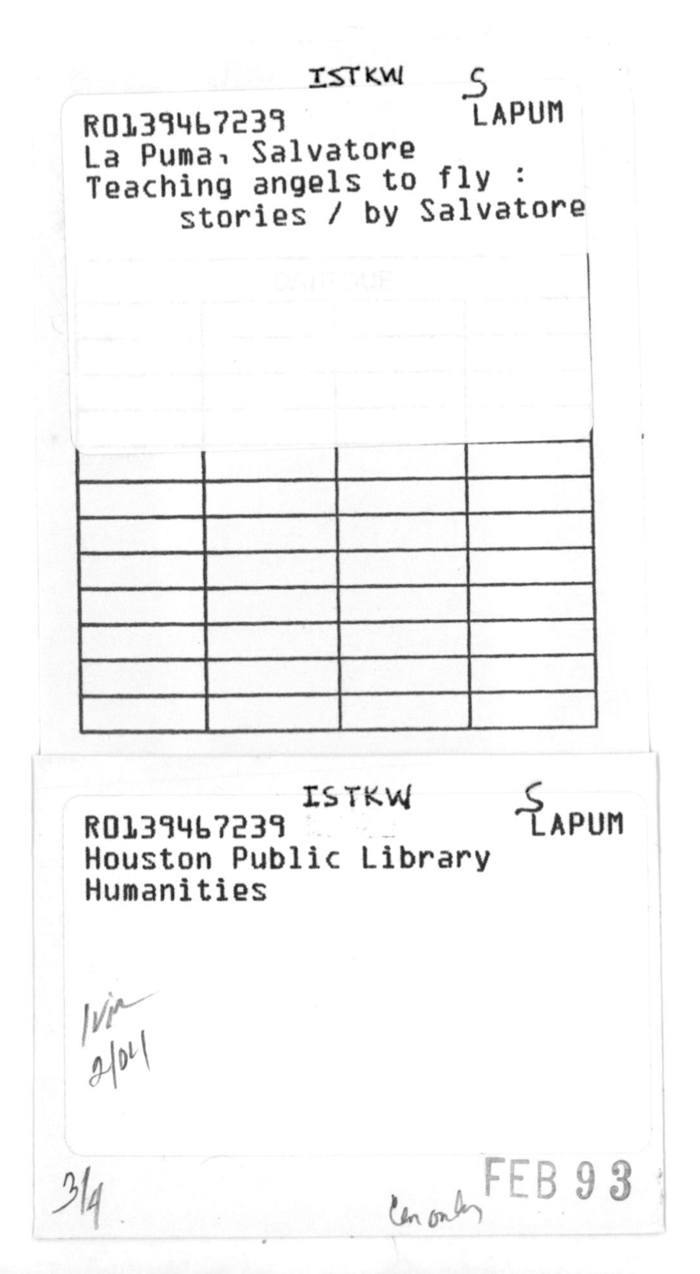